The HIDDEN SIDE *of the* MOON

The HIDDEN SIDE *of the* MOON

Musings of a life between India and Europe

by

Martin Kämpchen

NIYOGI BOOKS

Published by

NIYOGI BOOKS

D-78, Okhla Industrial Area, Phase-I
New Delhi-110 020, INDIA
Tel: 91-11-26816301, 49327000
Fax: 91-11-26810483, 26813830
email: niyogibooks@gmail.com
website: www.niyogibooksindia.com

Editor: Jayalakshmi Sengupta
Layout: Shashi Bhushan Prasad
Author photo on cover: Gernot Polland

ISBN: 978-93-83098-57-6
Publication: 2014

Printed at: Niyogi Offset Pvt. Ltd., New Delhi, India

How deeply have I loved the world,
again and again with each new life.
With my whole being I keep the world
in my embrace.

RABINDRANATH TAGORE, *BALAKA 19*

Contents

Preface

These short essays, first appeared in *The Statesman* (Kolkata/ Delhi). The astonishingly lively response they received motivated me to compile a selection of them as a book.

I was given a long rope by the editor, Mr Ravindra Kumar, to express my experiences and views. I am deeply grateful to him. There was no interference when I started to write on personal matters–on religion and spiritual life, on my life as a writer and as a friend of Indian village life, on my travels in India and Europe; there was only encouragement. Lectures and seminars on Indian cultural subjects took me to numerous countries in Europe and to the US. This and the continuous support of the Udo Keller Foundation (Hamburg) allowed me to travel widely and unhurriedly.

I found a format for my essays which is both subjective and emotional as well as conversational and philosophical. I chose my own angle of looking at the world which flows from my Indo-German background, from my idealism, also from my Christian upbringing and *sadhana* and no less from my search within Hinduism and Buddhism, but above all it flows from my love for the Indian people which remains vibrant even after spending forty years in this country.

Since 1980, I have lived in Shantiniketan; therefore it is natural that Rabindranath Tagore, the one great literary inspiration of my life, and the red earth of Shantiniketan are never far from my musings. Also, I never hide my closeness to the Santal villages around Shantiniketan in whose educational and social progress I have been involved for thirty years. Also, the Ramakrishna Mission Ashram at Narendrapur, south of Kolkata, has been mentioned often. I spent three and a half years there side-by-side with the monks during the earliest phase of my stay in India.

Introduction

FORTY YEARS IN INDIA

When I travel by train, say, from Bolpur to Howrah, people often ask me, 'How do you like India? How many days are you here already?' I reply in Bengali that I have long stopped counting the days. 'I am in India since 40 years.' The reaction I receive sometimes amazes me. Rather than erupting in delight about a white-skinned foreigner staying on in their country for so long, most fellow-travellers gape at me in disbelief.

'Forty years? That is a very long time!'

'Indeed,' I reply, laconically. 'Do you think I am overstaying?'

Only after that rhetorical question do my interlocutors resume their welcoming mode of conversation, common to most Bengalis. But I do not blame them for their reaction. My life's journey has not been the normal kind. It is difficult to understand how somebody from Europe who could have had a comfortable life with a career as an academician or a journalist and writer, would stay on in India beyond a few years. Those who do stay, mostly women, marry and start a family. Others are associated with a company or a university and do business or teach. But somebody, like me, who has never been married nor employed, neither in Europe nor in India, and never has held any academic position, to stay on as a freelancing writer, translator and cultural journalist, is, indeed, strange.

Often, I ask myself: How did it happen? It was certainly not planned that way. And it was not at all easy to tread this path. It needed sacrifices on the personal and professional levels, patience and strength to persevere. Yet, I have never regretted having spent almost my entire adult life in India. I cannot imagine another life but the one I have lived ... But let me start from the beginning.

Coming to India has not been a dream come true. As a school-going boy, I desperately wanted to visit Africa. I read books on West and East Africa and befriended students from Nigeria, Ghana and Liberia. When I was just 13, a Goethe-Institut was opened in my German hometown of Boppard, which is situated on the Rhine river overlooking a majestic bend with vineyards and woods spread on its slopes.

The Goethe-Institut—called Max Mueller Bhavan in India—invites students from all over the world to study German. Most of them arrived directly from their country and, in the beginning, felt lost and lonely in Boppard. So I stepped in, showing them the post-office, bank and bookshop, aided them in their studies and helped them to move on to study at a

German university which had been their aim. Their mentality suited me, their stories fascinated me and a great longing to visit their country overpowered me.

In the 1960s, it was impossible for a student to fly to Africa without financial assistance. Although my father was the principal of the Secondary School and College (a Gymnasium) in Boppard, he could not have afforded to gift me such a trip. He rather sent me, repeatedly, to England and France to learn English and French. I had to wait until I enrolled at the university to fulfill my aspiration. Every year, a government-subsidised organisation, Arbeitskreis Studien-Aufenthalte (called ASA) sent a group of competent German students, after a rigorous selection process, to a number of Third World countries. For three months, these young men and women studied the society of their respective guest country, made contacts with academic institutions and development agencies and then returned with a deeper understanding of these countries' cultural wealth and economic needs.

I was in my very first semester at the University of Saarbrücken when I applied for a travel grant to Nigeria. I prepared myself studiously and was selected. Then something unexpected happened. A tribal war broke out in Nigeria, the infamous Biafra War. One evening, I received a phone call from the director of the donor organisation informing me that the group of students destined for Nigeria could not proceed. Its members had to be distributed among the remaining groups. The director asked me, 'To which country do you want to go instead?'

I remember standing in a telephone booth (private phones were still rare) and spontaneously saying that one word which changed my life–'India'. I do not know why I said 'India'. At that time I had no Indian friends and had read little about India. I had only studied, intensely, Mahatma Gandhi's theory and the practice of non-violence. There was a reason for this: I had applied for the status of a 'Conscientious Objector'.

Military service was then still compulsory, so German youths were drafted into the army at eighteen. But I objected to serve in the army because this was the same as agreeing to carry a weapon and be ready to kill in the event of a war. The German government provided an alternative service for objectors like me (in hospitals, old-age homes and kindergartens, for example), but before being recognised as a conscientious objector, the applicants had to appear before a tribunal of the Defense Ministry and prove the genuineness of their conviction.

Many young objectors were not accepted. Some just wanted to get around the drudgery of military service. I prepared myself carefully, reading Mahatma Gandhi so as to present valid arguments against war and violence. My parents and my teachers opposed my decision, but I persevered and was given the status of a Conscientious Objector. This was before the beginning of the Vietnam War, during which the opposition to violence became much more widespread in Germany and other western countries. This, then, had been my only connection with India. But once I had said 'India', I began preparing myself for the three-month study tour with gusto.

When we, a group of five students, arrived in Bombay in the summer of 1971, we spent the first night in a decrepit hotel to which the taxi driver had taken us from the airport. After taking a shower in the evening my skin began itching from the sultry weather. It felt as if a horrible disease was creeping across my body. I thought I would not live to see the next day. Well, I did, and a few days later the group shifted to the home of an upper-class gentleman with whom we had established contact before our departure. The soft-footed servant boy impressed me. The dignified splendour prevailing in that majestic flat, which shut off all the noises and smells of the city, dazzled me.

Yet, I wanted to take in all the noises and smells! I craved to see and hear and touch it all. It was a delight to take the crowded suburban trains or the buses, to walk with hundreds of others on the roads. People stopped me to ask questions, and I replied, walked into their houses, made quick friendships and was ensnared and thrilled by the utter directness, simplicity and openness of communication.

In Europe, I had experienced the guarded and subdued manner of communication, tied to a number of rules, and was innocently unaware that any other manner was also viable. I realised that such immediacy of connecting with others was really what I had longed for. Much later, when I began to live in India, I also understood the negative side of such spontaneity—the invasion of privacy, the nagging omnipresence of people and noises.

After ten days in Bombay, I said goodbye to the other members of my group as I needed to travel alone to sense the pulse of Indian life. I travelled in a third class train compartment to Kolkata. This meant living in the same compartment with a few dozen people for two days and two nights. What better education in Indian life can one think of!

I arrived at Howrah station with a fistful of addresses. First, I put up with the family of a high-ranking police officer whose brother I had met in Germany. After a week, I shifted to the Ramakrishna Mission Institute of Culture. Its founder, Swami Nityaswarupananda, was in charge. I had brought with me a letter of introduction by the son of the famous German philosopher (and friend of Rabindranath Tagore), Count Hermann Keyserling. I had met Arnold Keyserling and his wife in Vienna, had told them of my impending visit to India and they dispatched me with introductions and rich blessings. Through him, I also established contact with the family of Netaji Subhash Chandra Bose and his circle.

It was the time Kolkata was plagued by the Naxalite onslaught. I was warned and admonished not to move around alone and not to walk on empty and dark roads. But I could not care less, because I saw no danger. Everybody was so friendly and welcoming! In fact, I never faced any trouble.

From Kolkata I travelled south–to Madras, Cochin, Quilon, Trivandrum, Kanyakumari. Then to Hyderabad, Bangalore, Coimbatore, back to Madras and to Kolkata. All by train and bus, staying mostly with families and in ashrams of the Ramakrishna Mission. After spending a few more days in Kolkata, I proceeded to Varanasi and Delhi and from there returned to Europe. While revisiting my new friends in

Kolkata, I already promised them that I would be back. They may have put this down as the ramblings of an overenthusiastic youngster, but Swami Nityaswarupananda offered me the post of a German teacher, and I was confident that I would keep my promise.

THE HIDDEN SIDE OF THE MOON

I have often tried to describe the initial impact India had on me, and each time I have to struggle to choose my words. I had grown up in two different places in Germany, had travelled to England and France with my parents and alone; almost each year we spent our vacation in northern Italy, which is my maternal grandmother's birthplace. Further, I had been a student in Vienna, the US and Paris before arriving in India. So I arrogantly felt that I had 'seen it all'. Yet, the 'otherness' of India struck me hard. And instantly its reality resonated within me. I realised that in India another side of my being, which I had not known in Europe and America, which was hidden from myself, now came into the open. In a way, I became a complete human being after I encountered India.

I, therefore, liken the experience of India to the discovery of the hidden half of the moon. We look at the illuminated shape of the moon and unthinkingly confirm, 'This is the moon!' We are not conscious of the fact that the reverse side of the moon exists as well. My experiences in Europe and the US constituted to me 'the moon', until I realised the reverse side while traveling in India.

Rather than just staying back and plunging headlong into Indian life, I was, however, clear in my mind that I had first to return to Europe to complete my studies. Remember, this was the time of the Hippie movement and the Flower Children culture. Many young men and women swept into India to lose themselves in the India of their fantasies, destroying the bridges to their home country behind them. This option never tempted me. I saw no reason to reject European culture and my Christian upbringing. I always sought to enrich my personality with India, which I wanted to reflect in my life and work as well.

In Vienna, I completed my doctoral thesis in modern German literature on the 'Depiction of Cruelty and Inhuman Acts in the Literature of the First and Second World War'. The topic was clearly influenced by my choice of being a pacifist. In January 1973, I was ceremoniously handed my doctorate. In early April, I was on my way back to India. I assumed a teaching post at Gol Park and, accepting Swami Lokeswarananda's kind invitation, I lived at the Ramakrishna Mission Ashrama at Narendrapur.

Now I began to realise that visiting India as a guest and *living* in India were two different modes of existence. As a guest, I was always treated as the *atithi narayan*, the 'guest who is to be treated like God', extolled by Hindu scripture. I was fussed over, I felt loved, felt important. In no other country have I come across such sincere and vibrant hospitality. Yet, living and working in India meant that I had to integrate myself with the society around me and that the society allowed me to get integrated. I was eager to accomplish my part.

I had arrived in Kolkata with the intention of spending a year or two before returning to Germany and starting a 'proper' profession. I had wanted to be a journalist and had already received a job offer. Instead, I stayed on in Kolkata for three-and-a-half years and then decided to become, again, a student. While at Narendrapur, I had all day to read and reflect and meditate because my classes at Gol Park were in the evening. I studied the Hindu and Christian scriptures, ancient and modern, and ploughed through works of world literature. Then I yearned to understand all that I had read on India in a more systematic and complete way, hence my wish to return to university.

I enrolled at Madras University for an MA in Indian Philosophy. Indian Jesuit fathers invited me to live in their institute. For three years I spent studying, travelled extensively in the south and began working as a writer, translator and journalist for German publications.

One should have thought that after my MA it was high time to return home. I had worked and studied in India and travelled extensively. About seven years had elapsed, and I had crossed thirty. Yet, I still felt I had not fully uncovered the hidden face of India. I was unable to leave, although my father generously offered to sponsor me for advanced studies in Europe. I might have stayed in South India because I was quite enamoured especially by Kerala. But one consideration prompted me to return to West Bengal. I urgently wanted to learn an Indian language. Foreign languages do not come easily to me. With English, French and Latin, I thought my capacity for learning languages had been exhausted. Therefore, while I was unsure whether I would stay on in India much longer, I had hesitated to accept the burden of learning an Indian language.

During my last few months at Narendrapur, a College student had given me a taste of Bengali. Conversing with acquaintances in Tamil Nadu, in Karnataka and Kerala who had, playfully, taught me a smattering of their mother tongues, I clearly realised they were excruciatingly difficult to pronounce. Bengali came to me more readily, perhaps because of its stronger similarity with Indo-Germanic languages. This was the deciding factor for me to return to West Bengal. Yet, I hesitated to again make Kolkata my base because I became afraid of this rapacious moloch of a city. I never have been a city person, having grown up in a small town. So I explored Shantiniketan as a possibility and my endeavour was immediately crowned with success. Thus in January 1980, I started to make Shantiniketan my residence–and I still live there after 34 years.

MAKING SHANTINIKETAN MY HOME

Now the actual work of integration began. No longer was I under the care of monks, Hindu or Christian, shielding me from society at large. Entirely on my own, I had to face the rough and tumble of staying in Bengali society without the privileges a guest can claim.

My entry into Shantiniketan had been effortless. Within two weeks I had a suitable accommodation at Purva Palli in the outhouse of Dr Moni Moulik, who became my mentor. With a recommendation in hand, I had, on my first day, approached Professors Ashin Das Gupta and Uma Das Gupta, a brilliant historian couple and two exceptional persons. They decided it would be best for me to meet Professor Kalidas Bhattacharya, the renowned philosopher and former Visva-Bharati vice-chancellor, with the request to be my doctoral guide.

Without much ado, they packed me into their old black car and took me to Kalidas da, who received us with kindness and, then and there, decided to accept me as his PhD student. Due to his influence, the process of registration was uncomplicated and swift.

I wanted to compare the life of two saints, one Hindu and one Christian, and chose Sri Ramakrishna and Francis of Assisi, the iconic 13th century Italian saint. I began my study of the Bengali language immediately and finally read all five volumes of the *Sri Sri Ramakrishna Kathamrita* in the original, which I considered a requirement for my research.

I was not a typical student. I already had a PhD I was not a stipend-holder. In Madras, I had begun to earn my livelihood from my writing and my translations. While in the South, I had translated a book on India from French to German and brought out two anthologies. A German weekly made me its India correspondent. I was not so much interested in strictly academic studies meant for a limited academic readership than in the kind of essay writing which has an academic base, yet appeals to a broader spectrum of educated people.

In Germany, there is an established culture of freelance writing. *Privatgelehrte* (private scholars) are respected because they give themselves up entirely to their research and writing, living, often quite inadequately, entirely from their publications and lectures. This they prefer to becoming a university professor with all the enormous prestige and pecuniary advantage as well as the encumbrances and unwanted diversions this job entails. Further, Germany has the institution of *freie Schriftsteller*, 'free', independent writers. 'Free' means they have shunned employment to be free to pursue their art. In India, we have no such tradition. A gifted and intelligent man or woman with good marks from the university will invariably go for *chakri*. Those who fall short of getting employment will be considered failures. Business is a second option. So when I slowly grew older and still remained at Shantiniketan, people probably assumed I had failed to get adequate work in Germany and was just hanging on in India.

The truth is that during my annual home visits I have not once applied for a job; rather, I rejected several offers. More than most other values, freedom has been a motivating force. But wanting freedom also meant remaining unsupported, unprotected, without prestige. For decades, my writing had been only in German, so hardly anybody in India was able to read my essays, my fiction and my translations. I could expect neither criticism nor appreciation.

Being seen as a 'failed' person at Shantiniketan had its regrettable consequences. I realised that a person without a position, without a designation to his/her name receives scant respect. People in the academic community did not know where to place me. Many probably viewed me as a 'life-long student'. In the first two years, I diligently met professors and other residents of Shantiniketan in their homes and we had rewarding discussions. But even after visiting them three or four times, they would never return my visit, or send me a note, or contact me by other means. At best, they deigned to come when they needed something–an address, a piece of advice on Germany, a translation, a recommendation. It became one-way-traffic. Many people tried to make me their *sishya*, putting themselves up as my *guru*. But this was not the kind of integration I was looking for. I went out in search of friendship, of stimulating discourse, of collaborative work for the enrichment of cultural and social life in Shantiniketan and West Bengal.

I became painfully conscious of the fact that family matters most in this country. To have a father or uncle or mother or elder brother who, in some way, did something important or was the friend of somebody important, mattered. My dear father, who died in 1987, had been a respected college principal with several books to his credit–but that, of course, meant little to people in Shantiniketan. I was just myself.

No matter how close I became to my friends, no matter how much I supported them, their own families would always rank first. Having no family in India, I was often left alone. There were and still are notable exceptions, people who had the modesty to see me as an equal and engaged me in intellectual discussion. But on the whole, alas! I failed to make the academic community my own. I admit that I felt hurt. By now, the wound has healed. I am engrossed in my intellectual and creative pursuits in my room, in writing and reading. My social contacts are on the whole confined to the cordial interaction with the Santal community in the villages around Shantiniketan. During winter and spring, numerous guests from Kolkata and from abroad come to Shantiniketan to interact with me. Besides, in the last few years there has been a marked reversal with several academicians taking note of my contribution to Tagore studies.

IS MY LIFE ANACHRONISTIC?

The time when individuals from Europe and America made India their home to achieve a great work for the benefit of Indian society is over. And it is good that this is so. After Charles F. Andrews, William W. Pearson and Leonard K. Elmhirst, no other western personality has given shape to the destiny of Shantiniketan as resolutely as they have. Perhaps no other guest has been given the opportunity to do so. We have seen Verrier Elwin (whom I admire), Nicholas Roerich, Mira Behn, Marjorie Sykes (whom I still meet at Shantiniketan), Mother Teresa and several highly respected foreign Jesuit fathers in India. This generation of pioneers has passed away. The leaders of society now emerge from among Indian people themselves.

Whoever comes to India from abroad at this age is not meant to lead, or to establish something new–at least not on a large scale and a highly visible platform. Indians should and can accomplish this themselves. Also, the time is gone when by leading an exemplary life of simplicity and honesty a westerner can inspire a large segment of the Indian populace. Anybody who may try this in our time will probably face irritation or plain disregard.

The *karma* of westerners today is to be members in a team with Indian colleagues, to serve rather than seek power, and to hand over their responsibilities to able Indian hands as quickly as possible. Rabindranath's ideal has been that men of different nationalities work together as equals for a common goal. This ideal has been before me throughout. I have never betrayed it.

Only once was I tempted to return to Europe for good. That was in 1998–1991 when, unexpectedly, East Europe erupted into freedom. Its Soviet regimes fell like pins; the fragrance of freedom and creative enterprise was in the air. I felt the itch to travel through East Europe, witness this important moment of history and 'do something'. However, I did not receive that irrevocable call that would have allowed me to leave everything and depart.

It was a sacrifice not to live like a full citizen. As a foreigner, I could not officially participate as a member of any organisation, hold office in any institution, give shape to my ideas or share my experience in any committee. The climate has been harsh. The heat and especially the humidity in summer and during the monsoon make me weak and edgy. To escape the worst time, I normally spend May and June in Germany for my lectures, my research and my visits to friends. The unforeseeable and sometimes interminable power cuts have often succeeded in distracting me and making me distraught, and I continue to get nervous from the noise. The garbage and litter thrown in the streets and public spaces offend my eyes every time I pass by.

But, and this is a mighty 'but', my forty years in India have been exceptionally fruitful. Work went well. I feel inspired and stimulated. My relative isolation has helped me to keep my focus on my writing and translations. Book after book has appeared; translations of Tagore's poems, the *Kathamrita* and Vivekananda's lectures in German translation, stories, a novel, essays...each book is on India, its culture, its religions, its social life.

In my cultural journalism I have attempted to create a sympathetic and balanced, a sober and factual picture of India. My aim was to avoid these two extremes: the romantic picture projected by so-called 'spiritual seekers' who paint an India peopled with *babas* and *yogis*; and the picture of India as a country of grinding poverty and injustice. The totally non-sensational reality of India is situated between these extremes and is much more varied, more painful as well as more cheerful, more richly human than the extremes suggest.

In the last two decades, I have regularly written for the cultural section of Germany's best-known national daily newspaper, the *Frankfurter Allgemeine Zeitung*. These articles have helped to shape the image of India among educated people in Germany. On the other hand, my frequent essays for *The Statesman* have been a sharing of my experiences and ideas with my Indian readers. Uniquely positioned at the intersection of Bengali or Indian life and European consciousness, participating in both worlds, my perception of life perhaps appears unusual. Never have I received more feedback as a writer than from readers of *The Statesman*. I see this as a vindication; my forty years in India may, after all, make a genuine intellectual contribution to India.

I continue to live at Shantiniketan. For over two decades I inhabit the outhouse of Mr Chandranath Bhattacharya's residence 'Hindol' in Purva Palli. It is a small, old-style bungalow with four valuable assets: The room I work in is a cabin so small that no second person can sit with me to work or chat or do something else. That means, in a gregarious country like India, by dint of necessity, I enjoy the privilege of sitting alone and working. Second, it has a large verandah where I can meet my guests, both from the villages and from Kolkata or Europe. At night, I sleep on the verandah surrounded by the many trees and bushes that I was allowed to grow on the large compound. This wilderness around me (which is in manifest contrast to the manicured gardens of the Shantiniketan *bhadraloks*) is the third advantage. The final one is that Chandranath Babu and his children have assured me that I may stay on as long as I wish. Maybe another two decades? Which other landlord around the world is so generous?

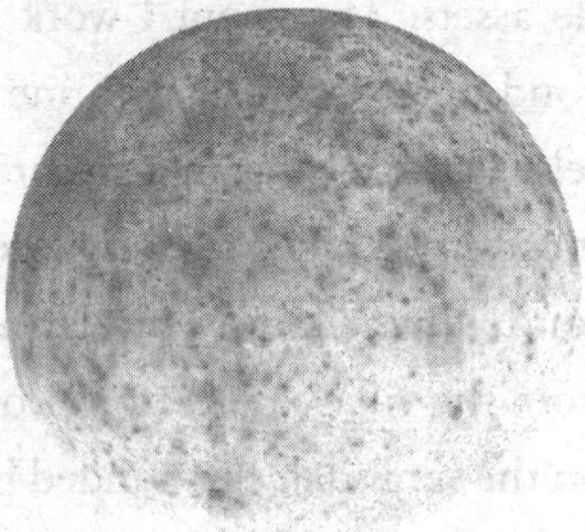

REFLECTIONS

Men reject the overwhelming mysteries of being
and jumble them up beyond recognition.
You alone know in this world
the primeval mystery of being.
Poet am I, this I shall forever humbly affirm,
and I shall replenish my spirit again and again
with the whole world's magic.

RABINDRANATH TAGORE, *UTSARGA 22*

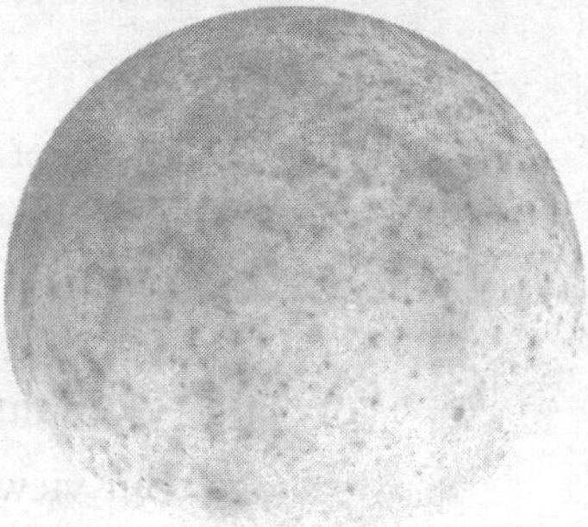

Celebrating Time's Luminous Flight

SEIZE THE DAY!

The ancients, so the Latin writer Ovid, knew that *nihil est annis velocius*—nothing is swifter than the years. Or, as the Greek philosopher Heraclitus pronounced: *panta rei*—everything flows. Especially, when a year ends and another begins, we wallow in self-pitying sentiments about the evanescence of time. How time flies! We moan. There are, however, signposts within the flux of time, like buoys in the river. Some are naturally given, like the day and the night, the cyclic waxing and waning of the moon, the seasons; some are man-made, like festivals, birthdays, anniversaries, and new years. These signposts are meant to make us conscious of the silent, steady, constant progress of time and tell us: one season gone—another season ahead; one year gone—another year ahead. There are one-time celebrations like births and marriages, like *annaprasan* or First Communion (among Catholics) or other rites of passage. But viewed from a detached distance these one-time celebrations, too, are mere repetitions of previous births and of rites in former generations. Each signpost in the river is, again, but one in an unending series.

Aware of time, its vastness and its flow, its interminable progress, sometimes our heads reel, overcome by wonder and anxiety. Like the French philosopher Blaise Pascal who, surveying the night sky, shuddered in mere amazement at the mysteries laid bare before him—bare, and yet insoluble.

We can take two different existential points of view. One is reacting to time by detaching ourselves from its dynamics as radically as possible. We can call time *maya*, and consider it non-existent, static, or repeating itself. This seems like a life-negating attitude, one preferred by votaries of an ascetic withdrawal from the concerns of material life.

Or, we choose the attitude of 'catching' time. *Carpe diem* or 'Seize the day!' is a Latin proverb. Once we conscientiously and with concentration try to use the time which every day gives us, we make one essential realisation: time does not flow at an even pace. It has greater or less intensity; it differs in quality depending on our activities and experiences. The most ecstatic moments—moments of physical and spiritual love, of friendship, of meditation, of the experience of beauty (but also of fear and pain)—intensify the experience of time. Such moments are often filled with *kairos* ('the supreme moment'), as Christian theologians would term it. They are redeeming moments which give us the power to loosen the fetters of petty thinking and trivial emotions. We feel the passage of time, but with an affirmative, positive attitude, because without time such ecstasy and joy, such redemption could not happen.

Rituals, seasonal celebrations, secular and religious feasts wish to accomplish the same–to infuse fleeting time with a special meaning. Yet, how often such occasions end in dead duty, in uncomprehending routine, in unwelcome expenses, in social obligations and, well, boredom.

But can we not create such superior quality of time ourselves, individually, or in small groups, and celebrate time's luminous path? I strongly believe in celebrating life every day and every hour–not just on special occasions. This can happen when we strive to become conscious of the gift of our life, and consequently, the gift of time. It will happen when we learn to assume an attitude to life marked by gratitude–for our health and intellect, our inspirations and experiences, our family and our friends, our professional activities and our spare-time leisure, our memories and our achievements–and, yes, even for our failures and disappointments as they too give us the opportunity to learn and grow more mature.

Further, the arts are a potent vehicle for making time more valuable. Especially, music ennobles time by intrinsically using it to achieve a desired effect. There is also theatre and other performing arts as also poetry and fine arts all, of which help us to appreciate time more meaningfully.

We can also create quality time alone–by praying, meditating, or simply beholding things that are beautiful. There are other things lending value to our time which rely on the interaction with others. Among them is one rare quality that may be considered most fecund in ennobling our whole life. It is a quality so precious that in the midst of the flux of time and its changing circumstances it gives our lives certain constancy, which is, metaphorically, a bridge across the flowing river. This is *loyalty and reliability*. It helps us to 'conquer' time by bestowing on it an unchanging, inexhaustible excellence, indeed, a taste of the eternal.

Gabriel Garcia Marquez's novel, *Love in the Time of Cholera* demonstrates this quasi-divine quality of loyalty potently when he tells the story of a man who as an adolescent falls in love with a woman whom he is finally able to marry in old age. But loyalty could be between any two human beings irrespective of their gender and relationship, be it a relationship of love, friendship, that of a teacher-student or a professional relationship. I remember asking my mother for a certain favour once and repeating my request a few days later. She chided me mildly saying, 'You need not tell me more than once.' She never failed me.

CELEBRATING DEPARTURE AND ARRIVAL

I spent some time in Kerala visiting its green coconut-groves and undulating hills, meeting its brightly smiling people that I remember from earlier trips. Part of the joys of increasing age is that wherever you go and whatever you do the memory of similar experiences or activities accompany and deepen your present experience.

But hardly back from Kerala to Shantiniketan, I had to pack my suitcase for an urgent trip to Germany necessitated by official engagements. Again goodbye, again a departure and an arrival. I do not, however, allow these goings and comings to unsettle me or, worse, to become a boring routine. They are, by necessity, so much a part of my life that I wish to make them a part of my life's meaning as well.

A week before a departure, I begin to prepare by putting into my suitcase, item by item, whatever comes to mind. In this way I am sure not to forget anything essential, and I am able to make my departure a celebration. Haste and confusion would be the death of any celebration.

Celebrating a departure essentially means the confirmation of human relationships, of their strength and loyalty and beauty. In daily life we interact with many people, both within the family and outside it, as a matter of course. When we depart we suddenly understand how much these relationships support and nourish us, how we depend on many of them for our mental and emotional health.

When we leave all these people behind, a feeling of gratitude emerges within us. How could we feel the pain of departure if that gratitude did not exist? Yet, this pain is also assuaged by the realisation that our best relationships will not weaken or change in quality through our absence. I love being given a farewell at home or at the railway station in Bolpur, or to be accompanied till Kolkata. I love being received at my destination. In India, friends have the leisure and the sense to make every farewell an event. They are used to meeting me at the railway station in throngs. But, please, do not discuss problems and difficulties just before leaving! I plead with them. It has often happened that discussions about our village work would continue on the railway platform right till the train began to move. This was painful for me, because I could not concentrate on the departure.

I attempt to be conscientiously friendly to the people I last see in India and the first I meet in Europe. In Kolkata, I make it a point to greet the people at the airlines counter whose business it is, of course, to greet back. Officials at the immigration counter or at the security, however, often hardly look at me. Only if they realise that I address them in Bengali do they pause for a chat and ask me where I live and what I do. In Frankfurt, the immigration officers invariably greet back—they have probably been trained to do so—but never would they get involved in curious and friendly questions. Baring a few times, there has never been anybody to pick me up at Frankfurt airport either. Even then, without expecting anybody, I catch myself looking around whether there is somebody to meet me. Each time there is a quick moment of disappointment.

When my mother died in September 2007, I was in Kalimpong and had to return to Shantiniketan hurriedly. Arriving at three o'clock at night, I saw two friends waiting for me. They had sacrificed their sleep to receive me and soften that painful moment of my life. When I proceeded to Boppard, my German home town, nobody was there to receive me at the airport or at the railway station. I took a taxi to my small flat, pulled out my keys and entered an empty room. I understood then why in India being alone is considered a curse. Indeed, it should not be part of normal life. I understood why social life is often richer in India.

Arrival should not plunge me into loneliness. Therefore, on the first day in Germany I often visit a favourite restaurant or coffee house or take a ride on my bicycle along a route I enjoy. This is well and good, but reconnecting to a place, first and foremost, means connecting with people and not with landscapes or atmospheres.

When I leave for India, friends in Europe ask: 'Are you glad to go back home?' When I leave for Germany, friends in India ask: 'Are you glad to go back home?' I am dumbfounded by these questions. Where and what is 'home'? Wherever you have good and loyal friends, is home, I often pronounce. Yet, I am unsure whether a place and friends is all it needs to have a 'home'. I am confused.

The definitions of home (*desh*) and alien country (*bidesh*) become all the more blurred in the age of mobile phones and the internet. These two devices have the one stupefying quality of doing their work without a fixed place. Your messages reach no matter from where you send them and where the receiver is located. Looking back on a complicated history of letters being addressed and re-addressed, forwarded and getting lost, I marvel at the convenience of mobile phones and emails. Due to them, I remain 'connected' with my Indian friends wherever I may be. No need for the celebrations of departure and arrivals anymore, then?

These celebrations are more necessary than ever! They must remain to assert the importance of the real over the virtual world. The virtual world allows you to send across your voice or your words, but not your body, not your *living presence*. In India the presence of a human being continues to be of paramount importance. You visit the person to whom you extend a marriage invitation! You visit the person you console after bereavement! Phone calls will not do. So, celebrations of departure and arrival do remain important.

Time has a Price

There is a fluidity of life in our country which is charming, often even inspirational. When a train arrives half-an-hour late, people say that it was 'still on time'. When a friend does not show up because he forgot (his excuse being he was not reminded), we are very understanding and say, 'Oh, he forgot', and that is enough of an explanation. When someone calls while we are in the middle of some important work or with other people, we simply excuse ourselves and take out time to talk. Look at farmers in our villages who need no watch because they have the sun for a guide through the day. Its position is enough for them to know the time. They rise with the rays of the sun and go to sleep with the fall of night. What is more natural? Daylight is for work; darkness for sleep, for re-creation. The perception of the passage of time need not be always mathematical, counted in minutes and hours, but by the importance of one's actions. Eating, for example, is 'intensive time', so is tilling the fields.

This sounds almost like childhood, where we were all innocent of considerations of time and space. However, what happens when the train does not arrive at all? What if that event is connected to a string of other events like having to catch a second train, or attending another meeting after the first one ended? What if maintaining time becomes a matter of life and death, happiness or tragedy? Then we are ejected from our paradise and dropped hard on the rocks of reality. In other words, as soon as we realise that we are not alone (unlike children who by nature are self-absorbed), but live within a society, within a context, the idea of timelessness evaporates. A common adage proclaims: The limits of our freedom are where the other people's freedom begins.

A sad commentary on our society is that many of its members try to manage this issue through hierarchy. They see themselves above others and therefore may arrogate rights which they deny to others and thus widen their freedom to the extent they wish. The most important freedom of being master of one's time can thus be compromised.

Normally time is cruel to the less privileged. Punctuality and unpunctuality are instruments wielded by the ones in power to their advantage. A politician or a bureaucrat can allow himself to be late by an hour or two without a murmur from subordinates. Others wait, so what! The message is: I am busy, very busy, while you have the time to wait and wait. Or else, why are you still standing and waiting here? The people who make others wait, may be subjected to the same ordeal by those who are at higher levels of power. They may feel humiliated, even outraged when their day's plans get upset, but do they realise how often they themselves have been late, unnecessarily causing similar distress to others?

Responsible management of one's time includes the ability to set priorities and to be honest about them. Punctuality is a virtue, no matter in which part of the world we live. Those who choose to be punctual desist from playing the games of power and prestige and understand the humiliation inflicted on others in being late, because they see equal worth in everybody. Respect to the socially underprivileged can be expressed best by being true to one's words and by being punctual. Sri Ramakrishna, though unlettered, made this a hallmark of his character, always abiding by what he promised.

We have looked at the lack of time-consciousness from the point of view of 'natural', rural living which has its distinct charm as long as it does not clash with 'modern' expectations and an urgency to make a living. Yet, there is another kind of timelessness, less connected with hierarchy and the dubious games of power: an unthinking carefree attitude, a complacent inertia or just the unwillingness to plan and engage in activity. People with this attitude do not react even when they are faced with the humiliating carelessness of others–the kind Swami Vivekananda castigated when he cried out, 'Do something bad, rather than doing nothing at all!' A life worth living begins with responsible time management.

Celebrating Life

Celebration calls for a talent to express oneself, to be extrovert, to communicate with others. Above all, it needs a generally positive outlook on life. Those who celebrate confirm by their very action that life is good, is worth living. That is one thing I like about Bengalis—they have a gift for celebration. The joyous abandon with which they celebrate Durga Puja and the plethora of festivals they observe throughout the year, proves this generously.

Even though no specific religious purpose may be served by these celebratory events they are of great import; an entire neighbourhood stays engaged in creative passion for some time, often healing social fractions and strengthening social values. Particularly, Durga Puja generates a great deal of bonding. The idols are conceptualised, their clothing made, the decorations thought out and prepared. This is followed by various drama and dance performances and a variety of shows staged during the four days of celebration which are unique to Bengalis.

I have experienced the most movingly beautiful Pujas in the ashram of the Ramakrishna Mission at Narendrapur. Their Kali Puja and Saraswati Puja were performed with that fervour which spontaneously pours itself into songs. Those *dhoti*-clad students rushing in and out to help the monk-priest and his assistants to carry on with their elaborate rituals are still vivid in my mind. Those long sessions of the most mellifluous *bhajans,* dedicated to Kali or Saraswati or to Ramakrishna, still ring in my ears. There I found a purity of celebration which cleanses the soul.

Unfortunately, the monks at Narendrapur do not celebrate Durga Puja in the ashram. Hence I often moved around in the neighbourhoods of Kolkata to witness the Durga Puja festival. As much as I took pleasure in its novelty for some years, the environment of perfunctory rituals and the show of opulence disappointed me. While these roadside celebrations display a certain neighbourhood unity, they also seem to dilute the positive impact and their importance by including Hindi film music, Bollywood style dancing, drinking and the display of sheer idleness.

My experience at the Ramakrishna Mission has led me to believe that a celebration when undertaken in a spirit of dedication can be nurturing and fulfilling. Those in the habit of working sincerely, with a sense of duty are automatically empowered to celebrate life more fully. Those who uphold and engage in the wholesome functioning of family and societal life, by doing so express a certain positive view of life and can truly feel the power of celebration.

There is, however, a powerful substratum in Indian life which appears to be life-negating. The path of the Vedantic discipline is the path of negation, *neti*. This substratum asserts that life is *maya*, an illusion, is unreal and should therefore be 'overcome' by a rigorous ascetic attitude. The philosophy that says life is given to human beings for realising their essential objective of unifying with God and therefore must be made full use of for that purpose is in danger of ultimately negating creational life.

If taken at face value, such a world view provides little cause for celebration. The one event worthy of celebration would be a permanent union with the godhead which is probably beyond any celebratory expression. The fatalistic lethargy, that all too common attitude of not even trying to succeed, the lazy proclamation of faith saying 'I leave it to God', without being active oneself may be attributed to a misinterpretation of Vedantic philosophy.

A life-negating philosophy is not for the many in society. Its adherents will always form a minority–the monks, the *sadhus*, the hermits. A life-affirming philosophy in its various forms will attract the many. But that does not mean that, sincerely put into practice, such a philosophy is easy or less profound. Both philosophies have their various levels of practical observance. At a superficial level, just as the life-negating trend may be interpreted as fatalism, a life-affirming trend may find an excuse to engage in gaudy, raucous and illicit enjoyments.

The worthiest modern-time exponent of a life-affirming philosophy was Rabindranath Tagore. He was not an ascetic; he wanted to praise both life and God and struggled, all his life, to formulate in his poems and essays a concept that gave room for enjoying both. His philosophy postulates that it was indeed possible to realise God's vision by passing through the troubles and tribulations, joys and ecstasies of a real life in a real world. This attempt to embrace the fullness of life to reach the fullness of God has given to mankind some of the most beautiful and stirring poems and songs. The poet never tired of expressing, analysing and evoking his belief because it possesses certain innate frictions and contradictions. So, Rabindranath had to go on and on expressing himself through various means to find a way out of these contradictions, both philosophically and emotionally.

Rabindranath initiated a number of festivals in Shantiniketan. His aim was to make these life-affirming celebrations aesthetically enjoyable and philosophically meaningful. He linked them to the seasons and their manifestations in nature. He wanted that his dance dramas and song-cycles enable their performers and listeners to lend expression to their emotions and thus refine them. The drama of human life in all its variety and complexity is meant to find a place in these celebrations. Whoever experiences them is expected to emerge with a refreshed positive outlook on life and with replenished energy to master one's personal fate. That is what celebrations are for. They are meant to be life-encompassing, rejuvenating one's conviction that life is good.

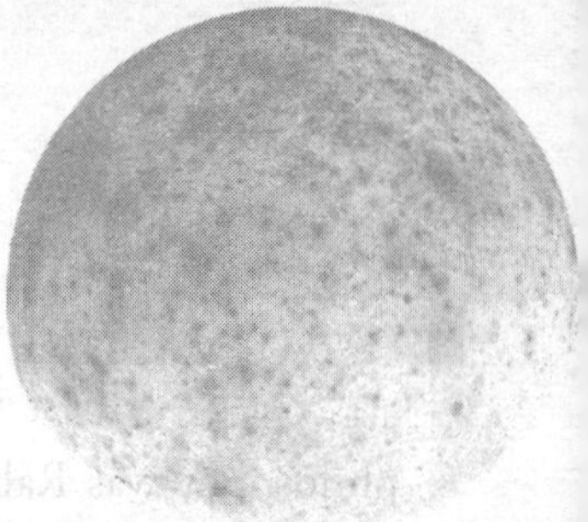

Innovating Rabindranath

It sometimes appears to me as if Rabindranath's works—particularly his poetry and plays—have been frozen in time by his followers. Did the Poet himself not experiment, say, with his stage productions, altering texts and songs until the minute before the performance was to begin? Theatre is an excitingly contemporaneous art form. It is capable of responding to social and political situations spontaneously. Why then do we so rarely exploit this flexibility in the case of Rabindranath's dance dramas and plays?

At Shantiniketan, only a handful of Rabindranath's dance dramas (*nritya natak*) are being enacted regularly. In the thirty-four years I lived there, many of his dance dramas were never staged. Similarly with his songs; out of over two thousand songs, I hear that just about two hundred are being performed. Can we not dig deeper into the treasure trove of Rabindra Sangeet and let the unknown songs be heard? Could the anniversary not be an occasion to retrieve the purity of the Poet's songs, singing them without harmonium and tabla?

Innovation can mean different things. It may mean returning to the source (for example, the renewed interest in baroque European music with original instruments, exactly the way they were conceived and composed). Innovation could also mean fusing the traditional with the new. If culture is to remain alive, it must encounter and creatively respond to and possibly even integrate ever new elements originally alien to it. This is, whether the purists like it or not, the way by which culture does not stagnate, but will remain alive and relevant to our contemporary world.

Rabindranath himself loved the happy eclectic mixing of his songs and dance forms. Yet, after his death a watchful university saw to it that the songs and dance dramas would not depart from their original mould. When the copyright was lifted, the entire œuvre was thrown open to experimentation. The vulgarisation of Tagore's aesthetic creations that had been officially feared, did not happen, barring a few exceptions. But the daring innovations that others hoped for also did not happen to the extent possible.

The other day, I watched a performance of *Tasher Desh* (The Card Country)–staged by Sangeet-Bhavan of Visva-Bharati. This is a highly symbolic play. A young prince and his companion are shipwrecked and washed ashore an unknown island. Its people follow rigid, artificial and mindless rules and disciplines, and dispense harsh punishments. Their minds are tied to the narrow confines of this life with no alternative to pursue. The young prince brings the breeze of freedom of thought and of action, gradually transforming the lives of people, ensuing a socio-cultural revolution and a more joyous, vibrant and meaningful life.

While such performances imbued with Rabindric energy and exuberance are common in Bengal the question that plagues one is why has it not been raised to a professional level where they would connect with theatre audiences outside Bengal and India? Few professional theatre directors, Indian or non-Indian, with international experience, try their hand at Rabindranth's plays. For one, the language is a hindrance. Besides, the special idiom of how its music and songs are to be woven into the plot which gives these musical dramas their special flavour, renders them nearly incapable of being transferred into other languages and cultures. With the enormous creative potential of Rabindranath's dramatic art forms, it is a pity therefore that his plays remain like caged tigers, unable to roam freely.

The play *Dakghar* (The Post Office) remains an exception as it has no songs, no mythology, and no allusions to the Indian social situation. It is a universal allegory, pure and simple. Therefore, this play has been internationalised in the past. 'The Post Office' is a play around the sick boy Amal who is not allowed by his uncle to leave his room. So a string of people come in front of his window to talk to him: the watchman, the milkman, some playing children and the flower-girl picking flowers to make garlands. Amal talks to each of them and through his zest for life and his positive attitude to each person, he instils a new meaning into everyone's life. Amal is being told mockingly that the king will open a post-office across the road he lives on so he can send a letter to Amal. The credulous boy is now full of anxious expectations to receive the king's letter. Amal's health worsens, and at the end the king indeed arrives himself, heralded by his messenger, to accompany the young boy from life to death.

The German translation has been put on stage in Switzerland and Germany by Wolfram Mehring. He chose a minimalistic form without props, not even a bed for Amal. The actors made just a few deliberate gestures and their lines were spoken slowly and with a ritualistic gravity. I have seen existentialist dramas like Samuel Beckett's *Waiting for Godot* being performed in a similar style. No throwing around of hands, no high-pitched voices speaking with animated velocity. The result was astonishing. Suddenly, the existential depth of the allegory could be fathomed. When Mehring was invited to produce the same play in Kolkata it went beyond one hundred shows.

The same play was staged in England in William Radice's translation. There, it achieved its relevance in quite a different manner. It drew from the story of the Polish doctor Janusz Korczak who had staged 'The Post Office' during the Second World War in the Jewish ghetto of Warsaw, for the children in his care. They were to be deported to a concentration camp. The play was meant to mentally prepare these children for their sad fate. The British production created a framework for the Tagore play which told the story of the doomed Warsaw children. So, the stage was actually set in the Warsaw Ghetto with its children performing 'The Post Office' and reacting to its message of consolation. Here, Tagore's play was given a new connotation by confronting it with a particular moment in history. The play's plot proved its universality by transcending its Bengali context and illuminating another context which was, originally, quite alien to it.

Just as 'The Post-Office' was adapted for the contemporary stage by integrating it into different relevant, modern contexts, the allegory of 'The Card Country' could also be experimented with. It can well symbolise a government office with its sometimes absurd rules and less-than-humane practices, or our Indian school system with its heartless convention of 'by-hearting' and insistence on grading. At a macro level it could stand for the fall of a country for example that of the Soviet Union 'overrun' by the spirit of democracy. I think we have a right to imagine and hope for such radical and creative innovations. After all, Rabindranath had similar experiences in mind when he wrote 'The Card Country' in 1933. That was the exact year when National Socialism began its dictatorship in Germany. There is no more horrible example of a rigid, military-style card country than the Third Reich in Germany between 1933 and 1945.

Considerably strong and new creative energies can be released when a story or an idea travels from one literary genre to another, or from literature to music or dance or to other art forms. Rabindranath himself has transformed many of his Bengali poems into (English) prose and thus created a body of texts so unusual in the English language that it earned him the Nobel Prize. In his Bengali œuvre he mingled poetry with drama, wrote narrative poems which became then the seed of future plays or musical dramas. Rabindranath's treatment of genres was fluid. He often wrote a poem and inserted it within the context of a drama, then made it an independent poem or a song. Rabindranath had little respect for the conventional confines of any genre, but rather he aimed at fusing all genres into a *Gesamtkunstwerk*—a 'total work of art' in which as many art forms as possible complemented each other, like the German composer Richard Wagner did in his operas. I am quite convinced that if Rabindranath lived today, he would not shy away from using video clips and special sound effects, animation and computer art in order to evoke his inner visions.

Although Rabindranath considered himself to be first a *kabi*, a poet, I think he was essentially a man of the stage. He naturally gravitated to the theatre because there he could unfold his multi-talented genius most effectively. He could write a play and act in it also, he composed the songs and the music of the play, and then he presented these songs on stage as well. He would design the stage props and the costumes or at least give ideas for them.

Being a 'primeval poet', pouring everything he experienced into poetic form, Rabindranath took an enormous delight in the spontaneity and evanescence of the creative process. He was a performer par excellence and probably felt best when he could conjure up his creative spontaneity in front of an audience. He sang for an audience and lectured for an audience; he wrote poems and found a special satisfaction by reciting them in front of people. In fact, in Europe it happened time and again that he recited his poems in Bengali without anybody in the audience understanding him. Newspapers commented on the musicality of his recitations, but obviously they could not judge their content. My impression is that this delighted him more than being a writer confined to the loneliness of his writing desk.

Why are our present-day energies not being harnessed to create performing events which develop Tagore's stories or poetic moods integrating them with the consciousness of our 21st century? After Rabindranath's death the first major transfer of his work to another form of art was in the films by Satyajit Ray and several other film directors, based on Rabindranath's novels or stories. It was a rare opportunity when the minds of two extraordinary creative persons came together to shape a work of art. A written story fills the mind-space with fleeting, shifting pictures of the imagination. A film, however, offers concrete pictures and sequences. While our imagination obeys our intuitive inclination, the pictures of a film cannot be evaded; they inescapably force themselves on our inner world. Hence the dictatorial impact of a film, as opposed to the volatile impact of a story.

Tagore's poems have been recited while a dancer 'translated' the poem into bodily movements. Narrative poems have been visualised as modern ballet or as an opera. For example, the ballad 'Debatar Grash' ('Snatched by the Gods') was transformed into a modern opera by William Radice who wrote the libretto and the composer Param Vir who wrote the music. The opera has been performed in several European countries and received high acclaim.

In Urbana, Illinois, I witnessed a small music ensemble hailing from Belgium which aims at playing Rabindra Sangeet on classical western musical instruments, like the violin and the cello. The Rajhans Orchestra has experienced professional musicians who play these songs according to staff notation. Mr Hans Vermeersch, the leader of the group, assured me that they do not omit a single musical note, truthfully following Rabindranath's score. This western approach to music-making urges the ear which is used to hear a voice, to listen to the melody afresh and thus to appreciate its nuances better. A voice normally carries more emotions than an instrument; hence with instruments the sheer musical quality of a melody can be fathomed, without listeners being overcome by the emotional appeal of the text and the voice.

In December 2010, I witnessed Tanusree Shankar and her dance troupe in Kolkata re-creating Tagore's poem, 'The Child', as a modern group dance. 'The Child', the only poem Rabindranath originally wrote in English, echoes his excitement after witnessing the Passion Play at Oberammergau near Munich. 'The Child' is idolised as a figure of cosmic dimensions. I am not fond of the pathos of this poem. Yet, seeing it enacted aroused different feelings. The dynamics of a group dance offered me a different view of the poem. The physicality of the quick and agile body movements downplayed the pathos and filled the poem with a more vigorous meaning.

To me it was a fine example of how a different art form can draw out surprising new colours and forms from a poem.

This, however, is possible only when a high degree of professionalism is maintained. If the transfer into a different genre means a degeneration of artistic standard, then the result will be popularisation, or trivialisation or even the prettifying of Tagore, no matter how sincere the effort to evoke a meaning within new forms may have been. Here, probably, lies the true challenge to the innovative spirit.

If culture is to remain alive, it must encounter and creatively respond to and possibly even integrate every new element originally alien to it. This is, whether the purists like it or not, the only way to make culture relevant to our contemporary world. It is my firm belief that by making Rabindranath Tagore's poems and plays and musical dramas relevant to the contemporary world by innovation, we could overcome the insularity of Bengali culture and also pose an alternative to the popularisation of Indian culture through Bollywood alone.

A Culture of Silence

At the end of every year when that all-time favourite Christmas carol, 'Silent Night, Holy Night', will be sung in churches and at market squares, in homes and on television all around the world, it will blare from microphones and make the silent nights shudder and drown in a sea of *schmaltz*. At Shantiniketan, the Christmas noises invariably mingle with the cacophony of the Poush Mela which with a hundred voices smother the *shanti* (peace) of Shantiniketan. In those days I seriously wonder whether contemporary India has a 'culture of silence'.

A casual observer of daily life will discover profuse evidence of sacred space in India. We have the roadside temples, the holy signs and little altars in old and well-shaped trees. We have hill-top shrines and holy rivers. Equally rich is the sacredness of time—for example, the specific times for *pujas* and sacrifices. But what about the sacredness of silence?

We are told that the *rishis* of the Vedas perceived God as one internal, inaudible sound at first which then unfolded into an audible, but subtle OM and further into the letters, words and sentences of holy scriptures and into song and music. A glimpse of that descent of God into human life can be captured, during classical concerts. Listening to the sitar often feels as if vast spaces open up to the imagination which plays and shapes and merges with them. One feels inspired and elevated and absorbed into a larger, a benign whole.

One would have thought that this experience of the sacredness of sound which is at the root of Indian culture, is being appreciated, in everyday life as well. Here is where my bewilderment begins: I cannot discover these traces. Sound is structured by its varying intensity but more importantly by its interplay with silence. So a culture of sound is as much a culture of silence.

When I was a child, we were told to be quiet when my father slept. We would tiptoe around the house and be careful not to bang the doors. When my brother did his homework, I was not allowed to chatter and play nearby. If somebody was ill, again silence was invoked because a sick person had to be treated with care.

With those memories in mind, I am baffled by the Indian resilience to noise. Children do not wake up when adults talk and laugh right next to them; it is a common sight that a street-seller peacefully sleeps beside his wares while the din and bustle of a busy street flows by. Shouting and speaking in a loud voice is not considered impolite; it is in fact part of the animated, pleasurable commotion that is whipped up whenever people who know each other meet. People do not actively object to or avoid noise intrusion, say, from car horns and mikes blaring songs the whole evening. Most people do not mind or just bear with it.

There are people who in fact need noise for their comfort. When I was a high school student in the US, I stayed with a family whose children would not fall asleep unless the TV was switched on. Some even fear silence just as they fear loneliness. Probably they associate silence with the negative side of life and with death. Silence haunts them. When I lived in Narendrapur, I was astonished to see that during vacation time the handful of hostel students left behind would move together. In Germany, I am sure, the reaction would be opposite. The students would be pleased that each of them has a room to himself.

This has a connection with the family life and the manner in which children grow up in India. They share their parents' room and the bed for many years and thus become used to the warmth of togetherness, to their elders' protection and to moving as a group. The price for this is the many tensions and confusions of family life; they can be overcome only by finding one's place in the family hierarchy and becoming tolerant to its demands. This includes tolerance of the constant noises of various kinds.

All of this I understand and accept, even though my early upbringing has not, physiologically, given me that hardiness to preserve my concentration and equanimity when subjected to long spells of noise. What worries me is that daily life appears to have no respect for silence even where it is genuinely called for. Here at Shantiniketan a dozen or more 'No Horn' signs were put up on the main road along the *ashram* area. I have not noticed a single person on a bike or in a car who would heed them. Whenever I pointed this out, I got a wave of the hand and a casual excuse. This is an example where the sacredness of silence is not even respected when demanded by an authority. There are other, more severe, instances where the lack of silence can be a practical impediment to success and mental peace.

I see noise as a killer of thoughts and feelings. 'Be quiet, I cannot hear myself think!'—this is a quip, but it alludes to the link between sound and processes of thought and feeling. Excessive noise can put an incalculable psychological pressure on us. In the long run it can impede one's mental and physical health. Those insensitive to noise are also likely to be equally insensitive to people and to many of the finer things in life. For example, can people with no need for silence truly enjoy classical music? Silence is generally associated with qualities of the human spirit—with prayer, with rituals, with sadness. In our present life in India, however, such mandatory or customary practice of silence in temples, or during death and cremation are rare.

What is important is to aim at a balance between sound and silence. I am told that deafness impairs people more radically than blindness. So sound is imperative for the happiness of men. Sound is never totally absent in our waking life; it adds to it a certain vibrancy, dimension and depth. I learnt this while helping with a documentary television film. The crew had taken a boat out from the Mumbai harbour to get a few shots of the city skyline. When they looked at the film material in the evening, the director decided to go out again. Why? They had forgotten to record the sound of the water. Only after those are added the pictures begin to 'breathe', he explained. A balance had been achieved.

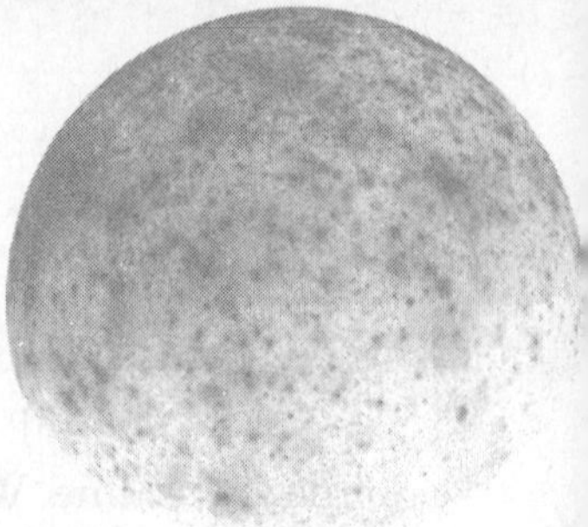

The Web of Life

Have you ever woken up at night, wide-eyed, become aware of the immense darkness around you, and felt a searing sense of loneliness? Surrounded by an empty space all around you with no lines, no boundaries, no light and no colour for the senses and the mind to hold on to; your life, seemingly, with no past and no future, no context and no structure?

At such moments I need to quickly switch on the light, sit down at my computer, write some letters listen to the radio or read a book. It is no mere attempt at distraction, but it is an effort to reconnect with the web of life that surrounds us so reassuringly during most of our waking hours.

This web of life embraces our family life and our professional life, it embraces our everyday joy of waking up refreshed and getting back to sleep after a day replete with activity. It includes being busy with our children and grandchildren, parents, brothers and sisters. It is so satisfying to be on course in our routine life that we fear to be jolted out of this habitual comfort by some mishap.

In western cultures, one is more afraid of loneliness than people in India. The psychologist Sudhir Kakar explains this as lack of individuality in a society where unity with the family is more important than to 'realise' oneself as an individual. Women and even men are capable of amazing sacrifices for the welfare of the family because there is no marked distinction between the family's welfare and one's own. Even in small episodes this tendency of staying together, to be group-oriented becomes evident. Taking a trip alone is manifestly no fun, only group-travel will make adventure enjoyable. There are examples galore.

While most children in India have the privilege of sharing their parents' bed up to almost puberty, in Germany we have our own bed right from birth, and later our own room, and we leave home at the age of twenty. If we don't, it will be suspected that something was 'wrong'. In other words, while we are raised with the objective of fortifying ourselves for a life to be spent independent, alone and on our own terms, on the Indian subcontinent children are trained to accommodate themselves in a group and be ready to adjust to larger families. Both are important techniques meant to lead to personal fulfillment. But none of them really prepares us for that existential loneliness that the first lines of this essay describe.

None of these approaches address or equip us to conquer such loneliness that engulfs us in a sleepless night; or, say, when a beloved suddenly expires; or love is unrequited; or when faced with failure or rejection. These are Moments of Truth: when the web of life is torn and that safety net is pulled from under our feet. We get the feeling of falling into a bottomless pit. At such times we cannot even look at ourselves; everything that mirrors our life looks meaningless; nothing that establishes our successes and failures, or reveals our position in society and our legitimate dignity seems to hold. At such times our imagination takes over and our 'demons' let loose from our subconscious. We have to fight them and fight them alone.

In that remarkable film *Life of Pi* (2012; by Ang Lee) where the young boy Pi has to survive on a boat in the Pacific Ocean, inhabited also by a hyena, an orangutan and a tiger, Pi has to battle them as well as his loneliness in the ocean. He battles these manifestations of his internal demons with an astonishingly wise combination of accommodation and wariness. Finally only the tiger and Pi are left on the boat. 'We need each other to survive,' Pi confesses. Pi needs the growling tiger, he needs his effort to keep the beast at bay, in order not to get lost in the vast loneliness of his life situation. And the tiger needs Pi to find food and a shore. Similarly, we need our tiger, our 'demons', to tear away the web of our conventional life and find what we really are in the stark, lonely moments of truth.

Here is a necessary interjection: no matter what we tend to become as a result of our cultural and family environment, whether we are moulded to be more independent or more group-oriented, we are as human beings meant for each other. Anatomically, emotionally, psychologically, a man and a woman are together meant to procreate, the woman is meant to bear children, parents look after young ones, and the elderly are supported by their children in return. A human contract and a generational contract bind us as a society. These are primeval bonds. But strange to say, the strings which tie us to our subconscious mind are, at times, more powerful. And the subconscious lands us into that loneliness which we so fear and try to avoid.

If you have a spiritual bent of mind, there is a further step to consider. Here comes in the term 'solitude'. At the face of it, the condition is the same as loneliness: being without company. But those, whose yearning and imagination go beyond the manifest world and seek to earn a revelatory glimpse of a transcendent reality, do need solitude to pursue this aim. They need to temporarily free themselves from their conventional life, their thought-processes and their natural tendencies. They voluntarily embrace that same loneliness which is so hard to bear when it throws itself on us unexpectedly. However, since seekers face that loneliness willingly and prepare themselves for its demanding existential rigour, they are capable of seeing its assertive and invigorating aspect.

These seekers are left with what Sigmund Freud so aptly called the 'oceanic feeling' which invades them after a while. We have Sri Ramakrishna's testimony, and Rabindranath Tagore's description and that of many others, regardless of religious affiliation and historical time, of this blissful side of solitude.

Pi's adventure adrift a tiny boat in the ocean, is a beautiful symbol, of this spiritual journey. The initial loneliness, the vastness of the experience and the bliss of finding oneself at the end, all are aptly captured by the ravishing beauty of the ocean. The moment of truth is revealed when loneliness loses its sting; when the need to be with family, with neighbours, with a group loses its urgency because everything is linked and gathered together in a cosmic connectedness which not only includes our little life, our family and loved ones but also nature, the sun and the moon and even our imagination. By voluntarily breaking free of the smaller web of life which smothers us, and learning to conquer our fear of being lonely, we suddenly find ourselves connected to this ever nurturing cosmic web of life and solitude becomes a reason to celebrate.

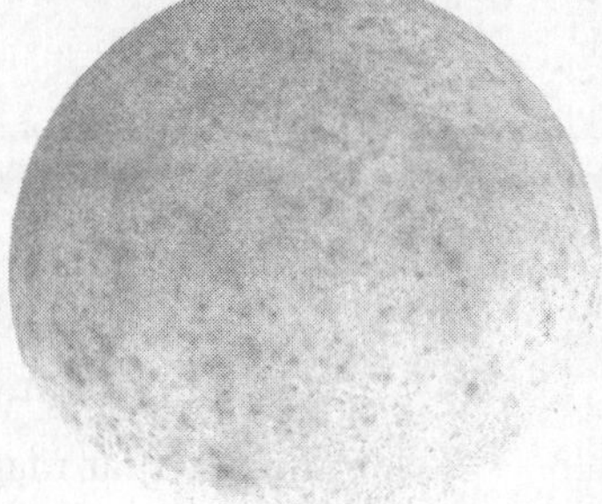

The Thank-you Mantra

In Germany and elsewhere we have routine ways of greeting, of pleading, of saying farewell, of expressing gratitude, grief or pleasure–signals which are culture specific. One important lesson to learn when one begins to live in another country, is to observe these signals and adjust to them. Yet, after a long stay on the Indian subcontinent I have decided that certain attitudes which I have imbibed in my childhood and consider meaningful should be introduced within my circle of influence. One such thing is the expression of gratitude.

In my childhood I was admonished to say *Danke schön!* whenever I received something. A spoonful of vegetables served on my plate–'Thank you!' A book taken from the shelf for me–'Thank you!' Whenever I forgot, I was reminded: 'You haven't said the magic word!' I grew up saying 'thank you!' for all small and big things in life. Looking around in Germany today, I find many things have changed, but parents continue to invoke that magic word.

On the other hand, in India I have been told time and again that saying 'thank you!' is a superficial routine. I have been laughed at and rebuked for saying those words, involuntarily, for the slightest reason. Indians give importance to *feeling* grateful and would rather not express it through words, which is considered mere lip service.

In India we cultivate genuine gratitude to our elders—to our parents, elder brothers and sisters, to our teachers. This is the *gurujan* ethos. We bend low to our seniors and are in most cases prepared to sacrifice time and energy to serve them, as a mode of 'repayment' (yes, without continuously saying 'thank you!'). This has been an important lesson for me.

Outside this narrow circle, gratitude can assume different expressions. Both giving and receiving gratitude is loaded with subtle problems. The 'giver' who expects gratitude does well to reflect: Have I ever made the other person feel that it is his duty to give me his time and services because I have helped him? Do I want power over him? Do I feel superior? Will I now remind him of my help every month making him feel strangely guilty?— Did I in any way 'burden' him with the 'duty' of gratitude? Indeed, these are the subtle dangers of being generous. Almost everybody expects some kind of return at least in the form of gratitude. Not to expect anything is an ideal few reach.

For the 'recipient' the situation is equally complex: To feel naturally grateful for whatever we have received is a wonderful virtue. Life is a gift—we should be grateful to the Creator God and to our parents. From this flows the continuous gratitude towards all those in the family and circle of elders and friends who have nurtured us physically, economically, emotionally and intellectually until we were prepared to nurture others. To feel and express gratitude is part of our progress towards maturity. Therefore, gratitude should and can never be a burden. It must be given happily and with freedom of mind.

Even then, the sentiments of gratitude often come with a covert frustration. In the eyes of the recipient, gratitude tends to belittle, even humble him. The consequence is that the gift or service must be reciprocated as soon as possible. Even if the gift is offered unasked and unprovoked, it may chain the receiver to the urge of immediately giving back. It needs a mature and strong mind to accept a gift that is freely given in that same spirit.

Genuine gratitude can emerge only from that strength of inner freedom. It comes from a mind that harbours no greed for more that is devoid of scheming and of manipulations and the impulse to exploit; and, above all, from a mind that in any given situation is ready to extend the same generosity that has been shown to him.

One of the greatest trials in my life, dedicated to the welfare of village people, has been to be tolerant to the blatant requests for more. Soon after I have donated one sweater I often hear, 'Can I have another one? My brother also needs one!' The rationale is: If I have the means to give one item, I can very well be prodded to give a second and third one. What is generously given is often grabbed with the intention to exploit the donor. I came to the conclusion that to expect genuine gratitude from people who are dependent on us, from our employees, servants, children, and from poor people, is generally unfair.

Expressing and accepting gratitude with genuineness is never easy. What is needed in both cases is the mental effort to put one's mind into the other person who accepts or expresses gratitude. This overtaxes many people who cannot muster such kind of sensitivity and imagination. The dilemma of giving and accepting is that indeed few can imagine and admit that it is an act without conditions, without strings attached. Most people suspect a hidden agenda, or a message. Therefore, offering gifts to people with limited self-confidence may be seen by them as a demonstration of superiority, even arrogance. We have a deep craving for prestige and dignity—for social status. If we lack self-confidence, it will stop us from developing simple gratitude.

Could the expression of gratitude be so difficult because it has no firm, assured place in Indian culture, outside the family and *gurujan* ambit? The theory of *karma* is generally chosen as a refuge in this context. According to this theory whatever we get is due to our accumulated *karma* from earlier lives. Consequently, when givers partake with their gifts they are paying up for their past sins and the gifts we receive in this lifetime are due to us for all the good we have done in the past. We therefore need to feel grateful to none but ourselves. This logic is possibly subconsciously ingrained in many.

Yet, can gratitude, or the rejection of it, really be a response to a metaphysical theory? If we choose gratitude, should it not be a simple outpouring of the heart? Instead of feeling a 'burden' or a lowering of prestige, a gift should infuse us with the joy of receiving, the joy of celebrating generosity in others and the joy that someone has considered us worthy of a gift. This ought to be the initial reaction.

Thereafter, gifts should indeed be an inspiration to share our life with others, rather than tying us down to some dire duty to return, in equal measure, what has been given. It should inspire in us a sense of togetherness, of companionship on the road towards a common goal. While it can instil in us the happiness that we are not alone, that we have the goodness of others to fall back on; it can also help us to develop that goodness in ourselves on which others may fall back on.

Gratitude can become an all-pervading feeling in us, evoked every morning after waking up. The gratitude to be alive and awake can infuse in us a positive strength for the entire day. The gratitude to be surrounded by good people, the gratitude to have work which gives us mental contentment and can satisfy our hunger and thirst and basic needs, the gratitude to have healthy bodies and minds, can ennoble us. In order to cultivate such a sense, I prefer to say 'thank you!' over and over again like a *mantra*. Do not our *gurus* prescribe that we keep our *mantra* on our lips the entire day? Not of course as a means to devalue it by parrot-like repetition, but in order to get it rooted into our body and mind.

Equality and Hierarchy

It is thoughtless to say that all people are equal, or should be equal. Obviously they are not. They differ regarding gender, age, character, talent and many other such characteristics. Apart from that they speak different languages, have grown up in different environments which offer them various opportunities in conducting their lives. But, equal they are, or should be, before the law as citizens of a democracy and before others as mature human beings. This entails that all human beings get an equal chance to develop their respective potential and lead a dignified life.

With a history of entrenched feudalism and a caste and class structure, we in India have taken to this idea of equality rather late and with some trepidation. The educated middle class bemoans the fact that traditional India is loaded with hierarchy, a tradition that lingers on. Being modern obviously means, to educated people, to cast away those shadows. And they point to the US where the practice of egalitarianism is supposedly far advanced.

It has been one of my major challenges to grapple with this issue. India's fairly structured social system depends on hierarchy. One factor is seniority. Older people are to be always respected and listened to, more than the younger. This gives importance to people with experience. But age does not necessarily mean that someone will be the best. The concept of seniority is actually derived from the family. In India the elder-most generation still has the final word in important matters, although it may not actually run the family anymore. Older people continue to be integrated in family life and feel needed which is indeed a wholesome attitude compared to the cruel marginalisation of the elderly in many other countries. But this could also mean ignoring fresh ideas and resisting change.

In a family, there can be no democracy. Everybody is either older or younger; either closer to the core family or farther removed. Some years ago, a twin was born in a family I know; a girl first and a few minutes later a boy. One would have thought that twins would be considered equals in the family. But no, the girl is addressed as *didi* (older sister) and the boy as *bhai* (younger brother) on the strength of those few minutes.

It provides enormous mental comfort 'to know one's place' in the family and, by extension, in society. It gives a warm feeling of being secured and sheltered. This allows everybody to grow, undisturbed by a need to aggressively shape their individuality.

Yet, traditional hierarchy must gradually transform itself and honour modern education and values. Here is an example:

a smart, energetic boy from a poor South Bengal village, one of eight brothers, was able to progress with scholarships until his graduation. He soon got a government job. None of his brothers achieved nearly as much. So the entire family began to depend on him for guidance and also for monetary help in emergencies. As a good son, he did his duty and lived very moderately himself. His elder brother's wife gave birth almost every year. Our friend was worried; he knew that he would ultimately have to carry the burden of this fecundity. Why didn't he give a stern warning to his brother or at least discuss the issue with him? He never did. 'How can I speak about these matters to my *dada*!' he maintained and indeed, later he had to bear the consequences with many sacrifices. Had he been able to assert his authority on the strength of his education and salary, life could have been easier for him and the entire family.

In some western countries, especially in the US, there is the opposite trend to level down the differences in society. Students often talk to their professors like equals, using their first name. Children, once grown up, address their father and mother by their first name, as if they were friends, not parents. There are other such examples. In western countries natural and grown hierarchies which support a person and enrich a relationship, tend to be ignored. Does a mother not remain a mother all our life? This should be gratefully respected. Those who have lost their mother early, can tell us about their deprivation.

I did not grow up with servants. My mother did all the household work and only kept a cleaning woman once a week. But in India I could not exist without regular help throughout the day. Daily household chores are too time-consuming as to allow me to dedicate myself to my writing and study. So there is Kamal, from a nearby village, who cooks and does my shopping, goes to the bank and post office and pays my bills. We are together since he was a teenager. In the meantime Kamal got married, and had two daughters who will soon appear for their matriculation. I would never call Kamal my 'servant'. He cooperates with me so I can concentrate on the work which he cannot do; I give importance to his work because I could not do it myself. I do not treat him as if he were replaceable. There is a symbiosis based on mutual respect. So when he prepares tea, he naturally makes a cup for himself also and has it sitting down with me. When I have guests, he naturally sits down and listens and, if he feels like it, participates in the discussion.

When some young men from the surrounding villages as well as guests from Kolkata's middle class come to see me at noon, I try to treat them with equal attention and give them the same dignity and even get them talking with each other. This is a challenge for both groups. It is an experiment which is not always accepted and which does not always succeed. From noon to 2 pm I keep my doors open for any visitors who care to meet me. I consider my visiting time a laboratory for such inter-cultural and inter-group activities.

I agree that these explorations into human relationships are loaded with complications. The person doing 'lower' work may exploit me; he may become conceited and unmanageable. True! However, my experience tells me that it basically depends on the character of the people involved and on the kind of bonding which is made possible. One may also argue that it is easier for me to engage in such experiments as my social status (as a foreigner) in this society is not fixed (and can take all kinds of shapes). Again, true! And yet, unless we as individuals and wherever we are placed in society break away, more and more, from the rigid standards of traditional interpersonal behaviour, we cannot think, speak and feel as modern human beings and act out this identity in other areas of our life.

Equality is an ideal which needs strength of mind and courage (as so stridently demanded by Swami Vivekananda). I have been aghast to see European residents of India (businessmen, representatives of NGOs etc.) who I had considered flaming democrats, treat their servants with haughty condescension making quite sure that they 'know their place'. This is the result of a culture clash and of insecurity due to language and social differences. True. But weakness of moral conviction is involved as well. Wherever we live we should constantly and consciously scrutinise and adjust our personal relationships to keep them equitable and fair and in consonance with our principles.

The 'Culture' of Corruption

We hear and read so much about corruption in public life that we can hardly react to any new revelations. The story is always the same: rules are all in place, but we either do not know them or do not care to know them, or blatantly ignore them; we are led either by mental sloth or a greed for unlawful gain to indulge in corruption.

What makes Indians so deeply susceptible to corruption, one wonders? It is not poverty as many of the most corrupt are fairly prosperous. Nor is it the feudal legacy which once allowed lords to reign over their subjects with brazen irreverence to dignity and justice. Why are people so prone to corruption especially when they love to be called the most religious people on earth and do indeed spend an enormous amount of time, emotional energy and wealth worshipping and practicing their faith?

These questions have haunted me for decades. My conclusion is that it is both sociological and psychological. Let me compare: In Europe, from early life we are fashioned into individuals. Soon after birth, babies get their own bed, they learn not to wet it and eat with their own hands. They are told not to cry and quarrel and not to interfere in the lives of adults. When the mother or father speaks, the children must respect them and keep quiet. They are given their clear limits and an unmistakable concept of what is right and what is wrong. 'Yes' for them is a yes, and 'No' remains a no. Punishment is always a possibility. Such an education is, however, not cruel, but is propelled by parental love, part of which is oriented towards equipping children to live in a society.

Not so in India where small children tend to be treated as if they still live in their mother's womb. Body contact with the mother is a must. Mothers feed their children with their hand often until they are ten years old or more. They are indulged in, and are allowed to occupy large spaces of the adults' attention and their private lives.

The result is that Indian children remain dependent on adult members of the family for a very long time, often until they themselves become parents. They tend to lack a pioneering spirit, a spirit of risk-taking and prefer to remain conservative (in the best sense of the word) and tradition-bound. They, however, enjoy enormous emotional security and a kind of primeval self-confidence or *Urvertrauen*, a term known in German psychology to refer to a child's primordial trust. This is supposed to shape and influence the psyche of a person throughout the life, often allowing one to endure a great deal of hardship with little emotional harm.

A European child, on the other hand, will venture out, leaving the sheltered life of the family as soon as possible. I remember that I went to England on my own when I was just fourteen, and to the US when sixteen. Nobody saw it as an act of extreme fortitude. We were expected to stand on our own feet and develop our potentialities, for which all possible help and guidance were offered. Yet, the emotional warmth that Indian children grow up with was never ours.

What does this have to do with the problem of corruption? It seems to me that in India the question of what is right and wrong, of what deserves a 'yes' and what deserves a 'no', is engulfed in a cloud of uncertainty. The decisions of what is right or wrong are largely not made according to clear objective norms, but by subjective examples, by family traditions enacted around the child. These examples and traditions can change and assume different shades of meaning according to altered situations. Right and wrong are therefore seen as something subjective and situational. This provides a massive grey area in private as well as public life which may not have the moorings of a personal value system or be guided by universal dos and don'ts. This area is unstructured. Norms and structures may indeed exist, but only on paper, for namesake. If even the respected and honoured persons of a family and of society at large neglect adhering to these norms, not following them is not shameful for the general population. One will take decisions on what to do in a given context according to the examples set by the family and the immediate social environment, with little consideration for social norms and laws. This group loyalty is at the origin of corruption. It tolerates that the individual basically looks after group interests first, ignoring the common good. Such group interests have different names: prestige, honour, security, convenience, profit.

Being guided by group interests need not have any criminal energy steering it. Bending the rules often amounts to a favour given to a family member or a friend, to honouring seniority and higher social position, to saving time and unnecessary expenses. Giving a bribe in order to be issued a passport or getting a ration card renewed, just saves the person a lot of running to offices and waiting for the clerks to do the job. We all know many such examples of actions which take advantage of this unstructured area of public life. It has developed into a kind of 'parallel system'. You ring up the friend of a colleague and he gives you what you need within a day. It is not the 'proper channel', it is not 'right', we know; it is exploiting the 'parallel system' which privileges us daily in many different ways. It is a 'backdoor culture'. It seriously disadvantages the unprivileged, the poor or the social 'lower classes'; true! Yet, inadvertently and without much thought, we flow with this parallel culture.

The real problem arises when this large, unstructured area of public life is exploited for criminal purposes. When does, for instance, asking for *baksheesh* become extortion? When does selfishness turn into hurting others? When does simply not observing a rule become criminal negligence?–one needs to be aware of the thin line that divides indulgent favouritism or simple negligence and criminal activity.

Crossing the street in spite of a red light is an everyday occurrence. This is 'right' as long as no accident happens. But when a child with less discrimination about traffic movements imitates you and is squashed under the wheel of a car, then your action suddenly is considered 'wrong', and people will even term it criminal. Yet, was it not criminal from the very outset? Almost daily we read in our newspapers examples of such behaviour which suddenly is seen as corrupt in the face of disaster.

In my opinion, corruption will end only when these grey areas, where neither right nor wrong exists, become totally unacceptable. This cannot be enforced with the formulation of new laws and the enactment of new controlling bodies. It calls for a new mindset–a mindset that respects the universal rights of all humanity over and above personal gains.

On Books and Booklovers

The annual book fair is an extraordinary event in Kolkata. I have witnessed the enthusiasm and fervour with which my friends anticipate the book fair. It is indeed heart-warming to see people so genuinely and zealously pursuing cultural activities. It goes against the image of the *bandh*-happy and politically overactive Bengali. It conforms to the counter-image of the culturally sensitive, artistically inclined Bengali.

Obviously, the prime target of visitors to the book fair is to see which new books have arrived on the market and to choose the books they want to read over the ensuing year. The annual book fair presents the most comfortable opportunity to do so. As most of our bookshops are insufficiently stocked, booklovers do not get an overview of what the market has to offer. When you have heard of a book you would like to buy, chances are good that it is not available in Kolkata, and you will have to wait for weeks to get it from Delhi or Mumbai.

The book fair is a wonderful alternative to scouting for books at shops or on the net. However, is the choice of books the only motivation to visit the book fair grounds? Let's be impartial: we want to see our friends and hope to be seen by them, especially by the culturally active ones who are into writing, and theatre, and are able to comment eruditely on both. It is the cultural chatter that we love to indulge in and be part of. It is mixed with feelings of solemn vanity especially if we have recently been inducted into its inner orbit: published a book or been part of a theatre production. Nothing wrong with that! Cultural talk is superior to political mudslinging or violent family rivalries. It is, let us say, harmless.

But should the culture of browsing, reading and reacting to books not be more than just 'harmless'? To read in order to be informed, to evaluate it critically, and to be able to participate in various discourses, is the duty of professionals who are meant to correct the course of thinking of others, to move the discussion to higher levels of reflection and experience, to help maintain and enhance high standards in culture and the arts, and guard people against all kinds of narrow, malevolent and sloppy thinking.

But for all others reading is to enjoy. It adds a variety of experiences which would have taken many years to acquire directly. The craving for pleasure is married to the urge to unravel the unknown. Books add new meanings to our lives, opens up choices. Especially fiction and poetry evoke new imaginative worlds which can then be integrated to make our lives all the more rich. The wealth of books over the years translates into a deeper human maturity, into a more profound understanding of and an empathy with the human condition. Reading usually culminates in the discovery of certain enduring values with which, at the end, one is happy to have lived by and is content to die with. Such meaningful reading habits radiate to the outside world in a well grounded and mature perspective on life. Reading can transcend our need to escape from the ordinary life and educate us to being open-minded and socially competent beings.

A book fair is obviously just a launching pad for cultivating such habits and can be considered only an extention to the joy of reading a book alone. Reading is per se an uncommunicative habit. The worth of a book lies in the transformational impact it has on us. It is that one poem, that one sentence, that one short story or that one novel which melts the ice in us and sets us on fire with its compelling power to change us which is the greatest gift a book can give us. Once we are under the spell of that magic, it becomes irrelevant how many books we have read.

For me reading books, both fiction and philosophy, has been virtually a life saver. When I first arrived in India, I dispatched a box of my favourite books ahead of me. I could not bear to be without these companions. Till today they are with me. Not that I would refer to them often. But the mere knowledge that I can, at any time, open my bookcase and pull out one of these books, comforts me. They are the most reliable friends I have. When I travel, it takes me a real effort to tear myself away. Not because of friends. I can always reach them over mobile or email. But because I miss my books. So you will always find several books in my suitcase, even if I am away for just a few days. I may not touch them at all. But still they are not dead weight. After all, I *could* have opened them.

These books become a part of me in the process of reading them. I find it disconcerting if I cannot underline by pencil certain key sentences in a book. I make marginal notes and scribble my comments on the free pages in the back. It is not only my method of taking a mental note of what I deem important, but it is also supposed to bring back the content and mood of the book should I return to it later, even after many years. After having completed a book, I hesitate to give it to someone else because with these scribbles it has become such an intimate part of my being. There is just one thing better than being surrounded by some good books, read or unread. And that is, writing a good book oneself.

The Art of Saying 'No'

In all the years I have lived in India I have rarely felt insecure or threatened. Whenever I was in a difficult situation, people, known or unknown, rallied around me and helped me. Indians, and especially Bengalis are indeed at their best when a sudden crisis occurs; they heroically 'rise to the occasion'. This spontaneous sacrifice of time and offering all of one's immediate resources is a deeply lovable quality. This quality is activated time and again, especially within the ambit of family life which never remains free from emergencies for long. Such acts of heroism are routine in India.

In Europe, however, such spontaneity is severely curtailed by tight work schedules, time-bound duties, and unbendable rules. Besides, everybody is aware that efficient public services are in place for almost any emergency, and citizens are to take advantage of them. The spontaneity of public life in India, its family-like informality, attractive as it may be, has severe risks and dangers. Two days after '26/11', the Mumbai attacks on the Taj International Hotel, I was travelling in a night train from New Jalpaiguri to Shealdah. A passenger, unknown to the ticket collector, handed him a small packet with a name scribbled on it. The passenger said that this person was in a certain coach and requested the ticket collector to hand over the packet to him. The ticket collector readily consented to do the needful. Not even at that time of a high security threat did he for one moment suspect foul play. Had he no instructions to refuse any such packages? Was he not aware of the danger his action entailed? People in India, used to living within the mental framework of a family life, condemn the thought of suspicion as an unfriendly act. They see virtue in total openness and trust, and they demand the same from others.

When society operates on the model of an extended family, then society demands the same privileges for its elder, more powerful, more moneyed, more competent members as a family would demand. The natural hierarchy of a family structure is being superimposed on society.

This is the gateway through which innumerable privileges flow into the social fabric which may be exploited by the powerful and wealthy. We all know how important, indeed vital, 'connections' are. They are established first by ancestry. Being the heir of a 'good' family is an excellent launching pad for professional success and social prestige. A father with a government job or with a position in the corporate world makes it wonderfully easy for his offspring to beat unemployment and insecure or badly paid jobs. Political connections are compulsory. And as privileges rule a large section of Indian society, the need for excellence and professional achievement is not emphasised. They can be bypassed. I remember a scene at Dum Dum Airport in Kolkata. A woman rushed in when the flight counter had already been closed. She was politely told that she was too late because the flight was about to leave. 'I shall phone the minister!' she yelled full of indignation. She was let in, against the rules. We all know similar examples from our daily experience.

If a whole society, by and large, functions on these lines, we can well imagine what this means for national security. Highly placed personages view it as something below their dignity to be scrutinised and questioned. Their privilege consists in being considered above suspicion. It is the common people who are to be searched and questioned. I remember a news item which reported that a national political leader refused to visit Australia because he was likely to face the same procedure at the airport as all other passengers. Rather than setting an example that in a democracy nobody is above the law, the politician refused to go.

In India we fail to make this distinction between family life and the civil society. Family life is a space where trust and dependence reign with none to be considered really evil. Everybody is part of a quasi-mythic innocence. Civil society demands a different mindset. Self-reliance, strength, vigilance and a sense of realism are required. A strong belief in professionalism makes civil society work, not informality. It is unprofessional to trust people because they come from a particular family, or because they are dressed impeccably, or because they can talk eloquently. Professionalism requires the strict and constant maintenance of objectivity.

My impression is that Indians tend to intuitively react against such professionalism. It goes against their grain. Their instinct tells them that most things in private and public life take care of themselves by the 'law' of informality. Being idealistic by nature, they suggest that professionalism is less 'true', less sympathetic, than informality, and therefore condemn it.

Being thus disinclined to honour rules and discipline, informality often slips into happy chaos–into corruption and injustice. It becomes a fight of one against all others, of the mighty against the weak. The most appropriate example is the traffic on our roads. Most drivers fight for their own progress, rather than keeping in mind the progress and welfare of the entire driving population which, in the end, would benefit them as well. Privilege-seeking informality, thus seen, is not an idealistic vision, but is cruelly selfish. No other country has more road fatalities than India. I see this as a result of naïve informality combined with lack of professionalism which refuse to acknowledge risks.

We all know how Bengalis detest uttering the word 'no'. They prefer to say, 'I'll do it later', and then perhaps not do it at all, rather than firmly say, 'Sorry, I cannot do it'. 'No' is not a word in an all-accepting family environment. But civil society needs a firm 'yes' and a firm 'no' to steer a decisive course of action. This inability to pronounce denial has become the symbol of a society which cannot dissociate itself from the warmth and the security net of a family life and accept the reality as it is. This mentality refuses to understand higher security risks. This explains why even when there are metal detector doors in place, they lie defunct.

If we wish to preclude further terrorist disasters, our entire mindset needs a drastic overhaul. Even with all the security training imparted and appropriate intelligence apparatus in place, unless the mindset changes nothing will make much of a difference.

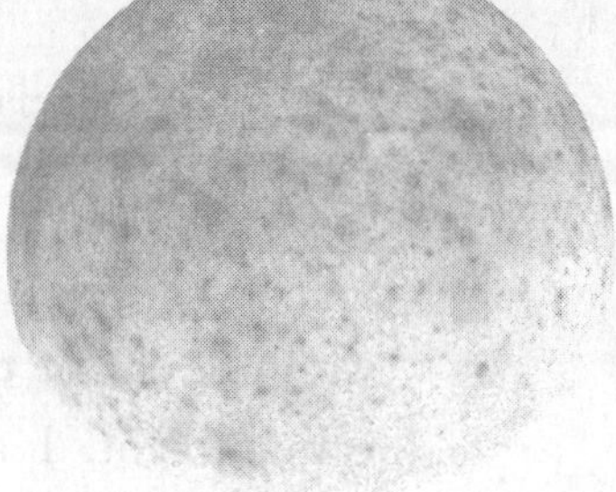

The Art of Communication

If asked what difficulty I face most in Bengal my reply will be, 'communication'.

Why? I would probably be asked back. We are such a communicative lot–do we not constantly interact with our family, with our colleagues? We are not even embarrassed to communicate with unknown people in public spaces. How can you claim that communication is a problem with us? We are so addicted to it that we even keep our mobiles switched on during meetings and events. One of my friends even answered calls while the Brahmin priest was trying to marry him off. Meetings are also constantly interrupted by ringing phones, and I am yet to see somebody who can heroically resist replying to it. Truly, communication is considered to be of overall importance.

The problem is not so much about communication itself as the reliability of communication. For example, whenever I receive an invitation, and after having accepted it, invariably within a day or two I get a phone call reminding me of the commitment. I am left wondering: Was such a reminder necessary? Do people think that I am so irresponsible that I will not honour a commitment? Or again, when I have promised to, say, write a letter, contact a person, or visit an office, the petitioner rings me up numerous times to enquire. I have to remind everyone that I will keep my promise.

These reminders do not point to an active distrust in my sincerity. A certain 'system', an unspoken understanding of how these matters are to be conducted, requires people to exert such pressure. By the same token when I make a request, I am expected to 'chase' the person (as the expression goes) until it is honoured. Such routine reminders and re-confirmations often originate from a lack of respect for exactness, for the spoken word. Why is this so? I have an explanation. The Bengali language has the beautiful expression *mukher katha*, which are words uttered without really meaning them. They are said in order to console or get rid of somebody or to delay a decision. Both partners of the conversation know that these words are said casually and perfunctorily. They prefer to say anything short of a firm 'no' just to make themselves and the other person feel comfortable. It reveals a certain parental softness and solicitousness, as the final 'no' is always so hard to bear.

There is another variety. Let us say I have promised a friend to visit him that evening. Later, he hears somebody has seen me on a rickshaw heading in the direction of the railway station. My friend automatically assumes that I have changed my mind, for whatever reason, and left by train for some other place. Hence, he is absent when I go to meet him at the appointed time. When I phone him up, he exclaims, highly embarrassed, 'But I thought...!' This 'assuming things' and a penchant to interpret the words of others, to understand what has been 'really meant', is rather common in India. Wanting to be helpful, we begin to 'imagine'. The result may indeed sometimes be helpful, but as often—see my example—it is not.

My personal explanation for this is that people in India are influenced by their age-old mythology. A 'mythic mind' perceives all facts of life in a web of stories, while the 'rational mind' views it as a series of laws, facts and logical deductions. So while a mind dominated by rationalism would strive to communicate with mathematical exactitude: 'A' is transmitted as 'A', a 'mythic mind' will tend to create a personal story behind every information received and include that while narrating the information. So, 'A' becomes 'AB'. As the information spreads from mouth to mouth, A' may be obliterated. I have always been fascinated by this special gift of storytelling derived from India's uninterrupted mythology. It is one reason why modern-day Indian literature in English is such a huge success throughout the world.

Communication in its original sense is direct, it is a person-to-person contact. The urge to communicate face to face shows that communication happens not merely to exchange information, but it has an emotional level. In spite of virtual reality—television and computer and telephone—making incursions into daily life, directness retains its value and necessity here. So if you wish to convey something critical or extend an important invitation (for example to a marriage) it is imperative to meet the other in person. No letter, no email, no phone call will do. The next best thing is the mobile phone which, as I have observed, has become a craze in a short time. But an email is emotionally not as satisfying, and I see many not taking it seriously as a means of communication and therefore not reacting to it.

When European friends find it difficult to, say, get things done in an office in India, I give them the following advice: first establish an emotional bond–take your time to speak of your family, of your children, of your religion, of your sorrow about the departure of a beloved one. Don't hesitate to sincerely respond to personal questions. Only then begin your official business. You'll see how much easier it will become. Such emphasis on the private sphere is indeed heart-warming as modern life tends to steer away from a regard for the personal.

This becomes dangerous only when the personal overrules the general good. This happens when corruption, nepotism, injustice hold sway and facts and honesty are being neglected.

In short, communication is more than an exchange of information and a conveyance of decisions. Further, personal communication has a creative side to it, at the expense of a definite structure and can be inseparably connected with imagination and private emotions. However, anything in excess tends to become unreliable and ineffective and that is when communication starts failing.

The Challenges of Multiple Identities

A month before Obama was elected President Arundhati Roy proclaimed in an interview, that he had to be 'whiter than a white man' to become a President. This is a dangerous juggling with words which made me wonder if escaping an identity was that easy or even desirable.

In my adolescence in the 1960s the struggle of America's black population for integration was at its climax. Martin Luther King inspired a movement which fought for equal rights for sitting in buses and trains. It fought for the basic human dignity of not being hated and shunned. I read the passionate literature by the black authors of that era, like Richard Wright's forceful and depressing autobiography *Black Boy*, Langston Hughes's mild and melancholy short stories and James Baldwin's eccentrically furious essays on segregation and wounded pride. I remember reading John Howard Griffin's *Black Like Me*, an account of his travels through the American south with darkened skin so as to look like an African American. He, a white American, wanted to experience first-hand what it meant to be black. The autobiography of the master of all spiritual singers, the great bass Paul Robeson, moved me and I began to translate it into German. Nothing came of it, of course. I was much too young.

When, at the age of sixteen, I got a scholarship to attend the senior class of an American high school, I was disappointed that the donor organisation sent me to Oshkosh, a smallish town in Wisconsin with no black population, and to an all-white Catholic high school.

I could not observe a multi-racial reality until I visited Chicago, New York and Washington, DC in 1966. I was not in the least afraid to pick up conversations with strangers in Manhattan and walk into the black suburbs of Washington until I was stopped and sent back by policemen. I naïvely felt that by merely watching and exchanging a few words, I would be able to understand and show my empathy—and make a difference.

Four years later, then a student at Vienna University, I again visited the US, traversing large parts of the country by Greyhound bus. In Manhattan I stayed with a western classical pianist, a black man, in his home in Harlem. I wanted to find out more about the life of the Harlem community and went to restaurants and bars with him. I still remember that we were accosted in crowded bars by young black men wanting to sell anything that could be transformed into a few dollars. They were drug addicts desperate for some money, I was told.

Yet, being constantly accompanied, I never felt threatened in Harlem. In fact, it was a tranquil place, quite in harmony with itself despite obvious poverty and social ills.

This experience of living in a disadvantaged community in the US had a great bearing on my desire to visit and ultimately stay in India. Visiting India while still a student, I was deeply curious about different concepts of life. How did Hindus fashion their lives according to their set of beliefs? How did poor villagers maintain their dignity and will to progress while tilling their fields? How did opportunities and obstructions in life shape the mind and will of individual people? Very gradually I became aware that there were no easy answers. I realised that in India each individual is burdened by a variety of identities. Family bonds define the common Indian's identity strongest of all. A common Indian is first of all, a faithful son or daughter, a good husband or wife and parent, a good brother or sister. Further, they have a clear and often painful caste or class consciousness they have to live with, then a village or town neighbourhood identity and finally, especially prominent at social and ritual events, a caste and religious identity. That means, typically most Indians accept the multiple identities that are thrust on them from birth.

So here I was living in India–a German writer and scholar, unattached to any institution, freelancing for German publishers and journals. I had no marked identity except simply being an individual. Or putting it differently, I was whatever others read into me. This proved to be both an advantage as well as a disadvantage. It was a disadvantage because people began to see me in many different ways which did not apply to me at all. I was just a student, I was a failed academic without work, I was a missionary, I was a hippie who got stuck in India, and so on. But it was also an advantage because people saw in me an outsider from their own often smothering identities, somebody in whom they could confide in and have access to consolation, advice and to ideas and thoughts outside their own circles. This combined well with my yearning for freedom, of doing something different, of following one's deeper intuitions rather than arid conventions. This became the pivot around which I was to begin meaningful and purposeful village work in two Santal villages outside Shantiniketan.

I was reminded of this baggage of identity again during Barrack Obama's momentous victory. Barrack Obama ran a non-racial campaign. He wanted to be President because he considered himself the best candidate with the best solutions for his country's troubles. He did not want to make history as the 'first black President'. His opponent John McCain was very guarded in not referring to Obama's racial identity as this would have been politically incorrect. Yet all around the two men the question was being discussed whether Obama's race would work against him and, if so, how seriously. Obama did not want to be a 'minority leader', but wanted to be an American who is capable of bringing together Americans of various identities under the umbrella of the 'American identity'. In this he succeeded.

While the election campaign was in full swing, *The New York Times* referred to India as a noble example of electing as Prime

Minister a member of a minority. The truth of the matter is, however, that Manmohan Singh, a Sikh, was not elected Prime Minister but appointed by his party. Neither was Sonia Gandhi elected to her post by popular vote. She continues to endure public slurs by opposition parties on her being an Italian by birth. At the micro-level, I as a European regularly face cat calls from young boys when I cycle to the neighbouring villages and a multitude of innuendos referring to my foreignness. Why? How I wish to be accepted as an individual trying to do a good job at whatever I was doing.

When I watched BBC World on the morning of 5 November 2008, I made an astonishing discovery. After it was clear that Barack Obama had won the election, all of a sudden everybody spoke of the great feat of an African-American becoming President. The opposition candidate McCain who had lost, dwelled on it; Obama touched upon it, though in a veiled manner, in the opening words of his victory speech; all commentators said it. Barack Obama was no longer merely the best person for the job, but his multiple identities had swamped him. Television showed African-Americans rejoicing all over the country.

I suddenly realised that none of us can escape our baggage of identities, no matter how hard we try. And we should perhaps not even try. As an African–American, Obama is the best man to lead the country. With the mixed baggage of history–his personal one, the black man's and the American nation's history–he will have to proceed to do what is expected of him. We are all chained by our identities and by the expectations others have of us due to these identities. In a reasonably successful life, the recognition we receive will transcend our identities. But for this to happen a lot of time, maybe decades, will have to elapse.

India's Mythological Tradition

THE MYTHIC MIND

India's mythological or narrative tradition has always been something to marvel at, something I have urged Indian friends to become conscious of and to cherish. People who have imbibed the two great epics are capable of continuously living on two levels of reality: on the level of everyday life, and on the mythic level which interacts with the level of everyday life. In the course of everyday decision-making their actions are directly informed by the examples of mythology.

Sixty years after independence, India is more than ever, at a crossroad. Does her thinking population sell itself wholesale to the temptations of modernity and emerge as the super kids of the computer age, or does it pursue and consciously continue with the Indian tradition which has been its mainstay for many centuries? Or is a wholesome, creative combination of these two mindsets possible?

In this context the controversy around the Ram Setu in the year 2008 fascinated me. The mythic Ram Setu which the monkey army of Lord Rama built from South India to Sri Lanka to save Sita from the clutches of the demon Ravana, was at the centre of this conflict. The coral riffs and rocks extending from Rameswaram to Sri Lanka are seen as remnants of that bridge, while scientifically speaking they are a geological formation, and not man-made. The government had been dredging a canal through that narrow passage between India and Sri Lanka, called the Palk Strait, to allow ocean ships to pass through, thus shortening the distance by 780 km. This dredging had entailed that the Rama Setu be partly damaged. In order to defend that step, court proceedings were initiated calling in question the historicity of Ram Setu and of Valmiki's *Ramayana* in which these events have been narrated, and, indeed, quite unnecessarily, the historical existence of Lord Rama himself.

A national debate had ensued when one particular political party was up in arms and began a movement in defence of Lord Rama and his bridge as a sanctified structure. The consensus that followed was that Rama indeed existed, and his existence needed no proof and that the Ram Setu also existed, at least as a mythological verity, and should not be disturbed. Only a few writers probed deeper, to gauge the difference between a historical and mythological fact.

A coinage by Romila Thapar was helpful; she wrote of a 'semitisation of Hinduism'. By which she implied that under the influence of western education, mythologies like the *Ramayana*, were being devalued as they lacked historical evidence. Proven history alone was being considered 'true'. The *Ramayana* and other mythological works are considered 'legendary' literature and not part of a documented history which represents 'truth'. The Semitic religions, Christianity and Islam, have a founder whose historical existence is proven and whose historicity is of the utmost importance to the self-understanding of these religions.

Originally, however, mythology in India professes its own form of truth which needs no props of historicity. Myth fuses the historical reality of various lives and various events into one complex narrative. Myth thus becomes condensed, heightened and intensified history. Rather than devaluing mythology as 'unhistorical', all Indians ought to be proud that they possess an unbroken tradition of mythology and myth-making spanning several thousand years. Even today the *Ramayana* and the *Mahabharata* are being retold and dramatised, altered and added on to suit different audiences and occasions. Had this spirit of legitimate pride prevailed in the present controversy, the myth-making qualities of the Hindu faith could surely have coped with the partial destruction of the Ram Setu. It would have at best created another myth justifying and explaining such physical alterations.

In India when people encounter new situations, they intuitively turn to the *Mahabharata* and *Ramayana* for guidance. They not only look for moral direction, they also want to fit in their own experiences into the social archetypes of mythology. By doing so, their own insignificant lives assume dignity and sometimes grandeur. Through myth, their lives become more meaningful; and through such meaning, their struggles and sorrows are transformed into something they can accept and endure. Personal struggles represent the eternal struggle of mankind, and personal sorrows participate in the eternal sorrow and pain of humankind. This dimension possesses a therapeutic and cathartic potential of consolation and release from suffering. People who dip their emotions into that ocean of myths return from it with a sense of sharing them with all of humanity and with all ages.

The Third Voice

[This is the shortened version of a speech delivered to Indians in the US.]

The enormous strain of making a decent living in an Indian city is to some extent softened by the mythologising faculty of the Indian mind. Equally, this mythologising faculty is a major factor for non-resident Indians to continue identifying themselves with Indian tradition, and for feeling an identity as Indians.

By 'Indian tradition' I do not refer to anything emotionally narrow and socially repressive. I mean something more expansive than 'family values' and 'moral values'; I mean a particular ethos: an 'idealising' tendency which is both naïve and pure-hearted; and a 'universalising' tendency which moves beyond history and beyond any narrow dualism of good and bad, and beyond the conventional distinctions of reason. This tendency makes the Indian mind deeply philosophical. Such idealism and universalism rarely move into abstraction. It remains part of the collective unconscious nurtured with stories of heroes and heroines, of gods and goddesses.

The most tangible element of that Indian ethos is its genius for narration. The Judaic-Christian tradition has commandments and precepts as its guidelines, while Hinduism prefers stories. It teaches by examples of heroism. It prefers the person-to-person contact when it comes to education. Storytelling originates in the family. A grandmother tells stories to her grandchildren which is highly valued in Indian family-life. Through stories, individuals become bound to the larger family—their linguistic community, their faith community and ethnic community. Through storytelling individuals become connected to the past—to their ancestors and to their gurus. In short through storytelling, individuals become emancipated into becoming members of various communities all at once. Through these communities they receive emotional and social security, they are tied into a hierarchy of cultural and moral values. Integrated into a web of stories, individuals are unlikely to be attacked by a feeling of existential emptiness and meaninglessness which so easily plagues a western mind.

It is indeed a great legacy, but also a special responsibility to possess such a 'security-net of stories'. This is connected with the search of educated Indians for a modern identity. From the time British colonial influence made itself felt in the educational and cultural field, literate Indians had to struggle for a proper integration of ancient Indian culture with modern European thinking. This balancing act continues until this day. The attempt at fusing Indian values with western culture is an epochal struggle to arrive at being a complete human being. Unfortunately, what is portrayed as western culture in India, is but the glitzy surface, is but the foamy crest of a wave. Indians in Europe and in North America have a better opportunity to delve deep into the value system of western culture. There they find not only Coca Cola and rock music, not only permissiveness and material greed, but below that surface they find the spirit of democracy, a sense of human equality, a civic sense battling for justice and fairness for every human being, a compassion for the poor and underprivileged, and a wish to preserve history and to learn from history.

Indians in the West have that unique chance to be what I call the 'third voice' of India. The first voice is heard from India itself; the second voice belongs to western critics and well-wishers of India; the 'third voice' is the voice of Indians abroad who have been nourished by their own tradition as well as by the tradition of the (western) country they reside in since decades. They have so much to give to both the West and to the country of their birth or of their parents. They should not give merely their professional competence as engineers and physicians, as computer programmers and academicians. Rather, they must combine within themselves the values of Indian and western cultures; they must manifest within their own personality that an integration of these two cultural traditions does indeed get them closer to becoming complete human beings. And with that potential of human completeness they should dedicate themselves to their motherland India.

Within a few decades India has moved from being a developing country to being mentioned as the new superpower of Asia. Its economic growth rate is a thing of wonder. Several social indicators have improved dramatically. The self-esteem of her citizens has risen inside the country as well as outside. Yet, all of us who visit India frequently know that projecting these features alone does not do justice to the present Indian situation. Poverty and inequality continue to be rampant. Particularly, the mindset of poverty has not yet changed. The 'third voice' in Europe and North America is vitally needed to offer solutions and the energy for Indian society to develop in a more balanced and just way. The first voice, namely educated society in India itself, is unfortunately often still too deeply embroiled in selfish pursuits of material happiness. Further, it suffers from that typical sense of insecurity which befalls people who have just recently reached material prosperity. To change this, the non-resident community of India needs to guide and energise Indian society in a much more conscious and determined manner than it does now.

In Rabindranath too, I recognise a 'third voice', a felicitous integration of 'Indianness' and 'Europeanness'. Rabindranath did not simply represent Bengali culture, nor did he belong only to the world. He evolved his own personality and generously gifted that personality to Bengal and to the world. The people representing the 'third voice' can learn from Rabindranath who, steeped in Bengali culture and moulding it, has nonetheless been a personality with whom other people of the world could easily relate.

One major lesson that I learnt from Rabindranath is that while poetry, songs, stories and theatre plays are certainly essential for a culture to become vigorous and to renew itself, of equal importance is to *act* in the spirit of the poems and stories we have imbibed. Creativity is a holistic life process which is not over after we have recited Rabindranath's poems or sung Rabindra Sangeet. Rabindranath built his Shantiniketan ashram and chose to live with the students and teachers of his school and university because such community living provided him with the framework to combine art and life into one whole. So, after our emotions have become ennobled by the narrative tradition we must live and act among men and women in that same spirit.

Diasporic Indians are in the danger of becoming conservative Hindus, Sikhs or Muslims. The lack of their accustomed supportive cultural and religious environment induces them to withdraw into themselves. They perhaps want to contain the entire cultural and religious wealth of their country wholly within themselves. Such insularity is positively dangerous. Rabindranath has spoken against cultural and religious insularity during his entire lifetime and with his entire life. Cultural and religious traditions can be maintained only by continuously evolving them. Culture and religion are not static entities. They can be living cultures and living religions only through constant change, only by always adding new traditions to old ones. The people of the 'third voice' should not fall back on insularity and conservatism to maintain their identity. They must give a positive shape to their individuality by creatively mediating between the cultures of India and Europe.

Poverty Among the Santal Tribals

For the last thirty years I am associated with a tribal village which is situated about eight kilometres outside Shantiniketan. I have learnt a great deal from the Santal community, and in the same way have I tried to give it all it was able to absorb from me. Over the years, we have in a joint effort established an alternative development which is not project-based, but wants to focus on the villagers and their educational, cultural, moral and material advancement. We have been clear in our desire not to build three-storeyed houses, but to 'build men', to build the characters of the young and the old.

It is a noble, but frightfully difficult, even perilous, task. Who can assure me that I myself have the noble and pure character that I want to see others obtain? By which means do I discern that I have the leadership qualities, the moral and intellectual balance needed to bring an entire village community forward in its struggle to lead a decent life? Two points are essential: First, while teaching others, my own desire for self-development must on no account ever falter. Second, I have in this long experiment depended keenly on my European value system while all the time remaining sensitive to tribal culture and to the tribal psyche. This interplay of Europe and tribal India has been a determining feature of our work.

Today I want to share my experience at Ghosaldanga and Bishnubati by discussing a seemingly 'academic' question which is, however, painfully practical: What does poverty mean? And how can village people escape poverty and reach a better quality of life? Unfortunately, we have learnt to understand poverty in abstract economic terms, by the calorie-count and financial graphs, or else from photographs that appear regularly in newspapers and arouse mere pity. A deeper understanding of poverty demands that we enter the minds of the human beings living in that state and try to see them, as much as possible, as they see themselves. This must happen simply, without the baggage of ideology or emotions.

Let me first ask this question: What do under-privileged village people themselves expect from life beyond sufficient food and the other most basic requirements of clothing and shelter? My experience is that their *conscious* demand towards life does indeed not extend much beyond food, clothes and shelter. They are gifted with a benign contentment with what they have always had and what they see all others in the village possessing. They enjoy a kind of gut-level, unreflected, instinctive satisfaction with what they have always had. A part of their condition of poverty is this lack of a capacity to *imagine* anything beyond their present state. This 'mental poverty', this poverty of intellectual, emotional and creative activity, can be alleviated only by (a) exposure to the choices they do have even in their under-privileged life, and (b) by formal education. I consider the ability to imagine something beyond one's own state, an *awareness of choices*, as the most important major step to get out of the 'food-is-all-we-need' mindset.

Apart from this conscious requirement of food, clothes and shelter, there are, however, several subconscious expectations among Santal village people which become conscious only when they face the lack of these needs. Among them I list three as essential: first, *a body healthy and strong* enough to perform its duties and to work and not become a financial and mental burden on the family or village. As long as the family is healthy, a poor person's life may be neatly balanced between demands and their fulfilment. But illness immediately throws such a life into turmoil. Expensive treatment, loss of manpower, lack of understanding one's own body can cause a financial and an emotional crisis.

Second, a normal, harmonious *family-village-community life* which supports the individual and gives him or her an important part of his or her identity. A vital ingredient of family- and community-life is a fully functional, happily performed *ritual life.* Poor people who are unable to fulfil their perceived ritual duties (to parents and elders, to the guru, to the spirits and to the deity) are indeed desperately under-privileged and feel worse off than even people who cannot always fill their belly.

Understanding this, I have never refused people who came to me for help to perform a family *puja*, or to do the last rites of a close relative. As a modern European who is a confessed individualist, I may have taken the line that these people should get out of their socio-ritual obligations which burden them disproportionately to their financial status. But I learnt that they prefer to move in tattered clothes, rather than give up their ritual tradition. It is this which integrates them into the social and metaphysical life-process.

Poor village people have a *deeply conservative mind*. Earlier my conjecture had been that poor people lack set values and fixed moral standards, that they are flexible and uninhibited by educated value-systems and by prestige thinking. The very opposite is true! Even and *especially* illiterate people imbibe from their infancy a certain value-system and a cultural formation to which they adhere adamantly. The conservatism of poor people in their ritual, social and cultural life stems from their inability, again, to imagine anything beyond what they have grown up with. It is a 'fundamentalism' which does not come from a discriminating conviction but from the simple fear that by non-adherence to these conservative norms, they may lose their very identity within society and their feeling of worth. Only with education comes the ability to differentiate between essentials and non-essentials and consequently the liberality to reject certain norms one has grown up with.

The third basic need is a relationship with nature and with *a space called 'home'*. This relationship extends to the fields, the trees, the pond, the courtyard and the mud-house, with the domesticated animals, then with the elements like sun and rain, night and day, and the great natural events like birth and death. From this union with nature and home and from a close-knit community life spontaneously evolve a variety of *cultural activities.* Most important are the festivities accentuated by dance, song, music, drinking and smoking. The tribals who lightly claim that all they want is to fill their bellies, would certainly not wish to sacrifice a pot of rice-beer and a smoke, nor dance and flute-playing.

It is with these cultural activities that the 'quality of life' begins for them. Watching the Santals dance, I am astonished how expressive and articulate they become. I realise that through these various complicated dance forms with their intricate rhythms the Santals learn to express their emotions of joy and fear, sorrow and protest. And by expressing them, they relieve themselves of the overwhelming pressure of these emotions. No education can achieve more with the inner human being than that, namely to teach how to balance one's emotions and how to have a healthy, realistic hold on life. These activities are, obviously, optional. They do not contribute to an income, nor do they stop people from earning their income. Santals may just as well desist from dancing and singing, as of course many of them, estranged from their culture, already do.

Having said this, I still realise from my experience at Ghosaldanga and Bishnubati that *formal education* is indeed *the* major factor provoking a leap forward with regard to quality of life. Such education is, of course, a two-edged sword. It teaches poor people to comprehend their own situation in a more objective way. On the one hand, they become intellectually enriched. But on the other hand, since education is not immediately and automatically followed by economic wealth, the result of education is often resentment and frustration. The students realise what they are missing due to their poverty. Hence, formal education does not *per se* lead to an improved quality of life. Indeed, the painful awareness education generates may also downgrade one's quality of life. Yet, education can just as well awaken their unknown inner resources and ambitions and empower them for the struggle to achieve aims like economic prosperity, increased knowledge and social position.

Education, as I see it imparted in the rural schools attended by the sons and daughters of poor families, does not really fulfil the requirements of education. Education should be an end in itself. It should unfold talents and latent dispositions and develop innate intelligence, apart from giving the keys to open the treasures of knowledge about the world around. But education as it is actually imparted, supplies knowledge packaged for achieving sufficiently high marks in examinations and ultimately grabbing a salaried job.

At the very least, education should teach certain skills needed in daily life, like boarding the right train to get to a particular destination, like not getting cheated in a shop or by an employer, like talking coherently to the doctor about your ailments and leading a hygienic life. Education normally does not take care of such rudimentary targets. They could relieve poor people of their all-pervading sense of insecurity in public life. If any one of our school-going village boys or girls does imbibe such basic skills, it is rather an accidental product of education, not one of its targets.

Education opens up a variety of influences and choices for poor villagers. Some of them are welcome, others not. Education stirs up more or less informed predilections, appreciations, aversions, desires and longings which students must integrate into their lives. Even very intelligent rural students will be initially overwhelmed by the choices they could make, but cannot achieve due to their village-based, poor life. All the enticing and interesting choices can apparently be redeemed only in urban areas. Many begin to dislike their village life and focus on its limitations, rather than on its cultural possibilities and natural beauty. At best, education *temporarily destabilises* poor rural students and it is entirely left to them either to turn their inner turmoil creatively into a life with enlightened choices within their poor rural setting, or to veer towards the conventional choices they can get in a city-based life. There is a third option, namely to return to their pre-educated lifestyle and slowly slide into a semi-illiterate state. Education as such does not automatically improve the quality of life of poor people. It all depends on what the students make of the education imparted to them.

Santal students have a particularly tricky predicament. Education to them means entering mainstream culture which is Bengali-oriented. Embarrassment about their own cultural peculiarities as well as the urge to integrate into mainstream (non-Santal) culture for personal advancement make Santal students neglect their own tribal culture, sometimes even disavow it. Education with all its benefits tends to make them rootless. Very few Santal students see the need and are able to nurture their culture and at the same time take a respected position in society at large. Chances are that he or she will lose out on one side. Few men and women from the Santal community or the non-Santal communities who are aware of the need for such a healthy balance try to empower meritorious students to achieve it. Has education provided these village tribal youths who have escaped poverty, with the quality of life they were looking for?

Can Anyone Imagine the Holocaust?

It is a matter of interest that fast-living societies dedicated to fleeting pleasures, such as Germany and Austria, are still deeply fascinated by their history. This is generally so, not merely pertaining to the recent history of the last two or three generations. Large, well-arranged exhibitions on historical subjects with a slightly popular appeal can count on a veritable flood of visitors for weeks, even months. For sociologists this indicates the urge of modern societies to be rooted, to feel and understand one's own roots in history. The interest in Third Reich and holocaust history is mixed with the sense of a haunting guilt. These are roots one would think dry and wither in time, yet they do not. To this day, war diaries and letters are being published, films analysing the evil genius of Hitler are produced. A spate of research on the Jewish holocaust, the establishment of new museums and memorials are part of an effort not to forget these horrors.

Once or twice there was a call by well-meaning intellectuals to tone down this 'cult' of remembrance, to let bygones be bygones and move ahead. Yet, each time a public outcry followed with an indignant rejection of these suggestions. Germany is the one country where it is forbidden by law to deny the existence of the holocaust. The official position is that the German people would have to remain forever ashamed and horrified by what had happened.

I became part of this guilt culture early in my life. I wrote a doctoral thesis at Vienna University on the literature of the two world wars and of the concentration camps. Looking at short stories, novels, plays, literary documentations, I tried to understand whether it was at all possible to depict acts of inhumanity and cruelty, realistically and truthfully within a literary framework. According to the classical theory, a text does not succeed in becoming literature without the application of the principles of ethics and aesthetics. Texts which bluntly glorify murder, revel in perversion and gory details, exalt in rape or sexual exploitation are bound to fail as literature.

In my thesis I have tried to show how descriptions of battles, once they take in every detail realistically, tend by their very realism to become an *approval* of these horrors. Or else, the descriptions become blurred and fail to evoke a picture in the mind. In other words, we can describe with literary competence only such situations of life which harbour an element of the good and the beautiful within themselves. Accordingly, successful literature on modern wars and the holocaust has so far not viewed its topics from within, from their very centre, but generally from the periphery.

This follows the known scheme of Greek tragedy where a battle is not being shown on stage. Instead, a citizen standing on stage describes the battle which happens off stage. For example, the daily activities in the Auschwitz concentration camp were famously evoked in the theatre play *Die Ermittlung* by Peter Weiss which portrays the court case in Frankfurt against some SS bosses who lorded over Auschwitz. Moreover, the playwright faithfully selected his dialogues exclusively from the words which were spoken during court proceedings. This points to the second rule so far followed by successful holocaust literature: It is strictly documentary, taken from eye-witness accounts or related from one's own memory. A third rule almost universally followed has been so far that holocaust literature views the atrocities perpetrated on Jews from the Jewish perspective, that is from the angle of the victims.

In 2006, a voluminous novel appeared in France, *Les Bienveillantes* ('The Kindly Ones') by Jonathan Littell. It totally overthrew all these standards of holocaust literature. Littell's 1300 page-novel is the fictional memoir of an SS officer whom the author names Max Aue. Aue participates in the German war in Russia, witnesses the battle of Stalingrad, then is part of the death machinery at the Auschwitz concentration camp and finally even visits the hideout of the *Führer*, Adolf Hitler. The French author who was below forty years when he wrote his novel, has not witnessed the war and the concentration camps. So his book is not documentary. He describes everyday life in the midst of war and concentration camp, so he is not on the periphery, and finally, Max Aue is not a victim, but a *Täter*, a 'perpetrator', a mass killer.

This shook the French nation. The French understood the monstrosity of the endeavour to imagine the holocaust. The questions being asked were: Is it 'allowed' to do this? And, does it amount to good literature? Or is the book merely a kitschy and unbelievable exercise of a sadist mind which deserves to be outrightly rejected? In the original French the book sold an estimated one million copies within a year and received the last year's most prestigious prize for literature in France, the Prix Goncourt. So it must be taken seriously.

To understand this unusual book, some facts must be known of Jonathan Littell. Though he wrote his book in French, his background is multi-cultural. The family hails from eastern Europe and moved to the United States. Jonathan Littell is an American Jew. He attended school in France, and studied law at Yale University. As a young man he spent five years in Russia, three of them in Chechenya during the time when the Russian government had launched a brutal war against an uprising in search of political independence. As a member of an international NGO working against world hunger, he also spent time in Bosnia and Afghanistan. With his own eyes, Littell saw the horrors of genocide, torture and misery. He then returned to write his book which had been on his mind since early adulthood. He spent five years writing it. He researched the mechanism of state terror to the minutest detail in order to recreate the Nazi Regime's functioning authentically.

Just imagine! A Jew identifies himself with a Nazi mass murderer, imagines his life and writes it down in a first person account! Jonathan Littell invented Max Aue who was convinced that the extermination of the Jews was necessary, a man who never felt any remorse of what he was doing, not even after the war when he moved to France and began to lead a conventional life as a family man and the manager of a factory. What is more, Max Aue is portrayed as a man of high cultural refinement who is well-read, who appreciates music and art. The message is that culture with all its humanistic ethos does not save anybody from becoming a cold-blooded murderer. This is borne out by some diaries of concentration camp bosses. After having sent hundreds of men, women and children to the gas chambers during the day, they were able to relax to the sound of Mozart and Beethoven in the evening.

The second message, not less frightening, is that 'Everybody is a German'. As Littell stressed in his interviews, he believes that there is brutality in all of us, and if the opportunity arises, all of us will become murderers. It may happen again in our time; it may happen elsewhere in Europe and in Asia. These are chilling thoughts.

As to the literary success of Littell's opus, time is not really ripe yet to decide whether or not the novel 'works' as a piece of literature. So far the reading public tried to absorb the shock that a contemporary writer did indeed cross the line and dare to put his mind into the mind of a mass murderer. In an interview Littell asked: 'How can mass murders be organised? I have met people who have murdered with their own hands.

But I continue to feel strange that in the heads of these people, there was room for love of their children and their family at the same time. They torture human beings like they are themselves, and children like their own children.'

Littell claims that there is indeed 'beauty' in his work, and he sees himself as an intellectual moralist. His stated intention is to show what exactly happened in the minds of individuals who were faced with the choice to kill or to desist from killing. 'It is very difficult to be a decent human being', Littell concluded in the same interview, 'In the West we like to believe that we have somehow struck a balance, but for the rest of humanity, life is a nightmare.'

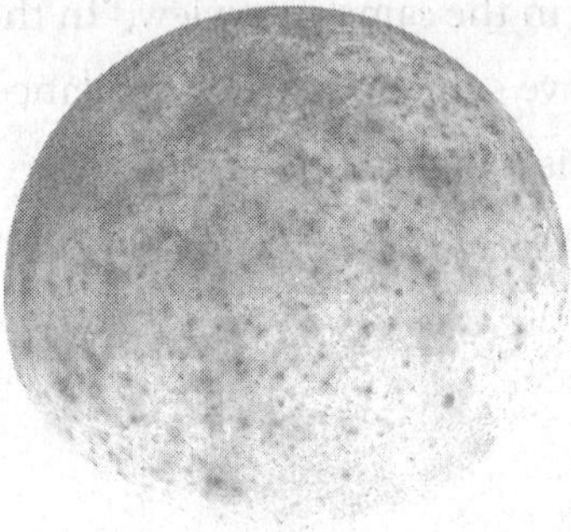

REMINISCENCES

But I, I want to see everything there is to see.
Roam about and *only* see!

RABINDRANATH TAGORE, *DAKGHAR*
(The Post-Office)

Remembering Prasanta Kumar Paul

I first met Prasanta Kumar Paul in the late 1980s, when I prepared my German biography of Rabindranath Tagore. 'Prasanta da' then lived in the annexe of the Ratan Kutir at Shantiniketan, shuttling between his college duties in Kolkata and his research at the Rabindra Bhavan. He was unassuming, almost rustic looking, without any kind of airs. We had many meetings in his small room in the evenings after he returned from the library. He generously supplied me with every detail from Rabindranath's life I asked for, mostly from memory. At that time he was sufficiently happy in Shantiniketan to want to shift to Visva-Bharati full-time. After becoming a professor at Rabindra Bhavan, he first stayed in the university quarters near the Ratan Palli market and later built a house in the Aban Palli area of Shantiniketan.

Prasanta da is the person in Shantiniketan I admired the most. I realised that he rendered help to other Tagore scholars, like Andrew Robinson and Krishna Datta, with equal generosity. His dedication and mental application to Rabindranath and to his life's work, the Bengali biography of Rabindranath Tagore, was without a parallel. I have seen many anti-models, intellectuals who are simultaneously engaged in half-a-dozen or more activities scattering their energies, rarely leading to a consistent and remarkable *œuvre*. In fact, Prasanta da once mildly warned me not to spread myself too much. He particularly alluded to my activities in two Santal villages at some distance from Shantiniketan. But after visiting me in my modest accommodation at noon one day, and seeing me joyously interacting with a few Santal youths who had arrived from their villages with various suggestions and requests, he realised I was not wasting my time. He never chided me again. I still remember how, sitting in a cane chair among these village people, he had such a good time exchanging banter with them. He was able to switch from his concerns about Rabindranath to village concerns without any problem.

I maintain a strict rule of not entertaining visitors before noon. The time before that is reserved for writing. The first time Prasanta da visited me, he arrived ten minutes early. Courteously, I made him sit on the verandah and returned to my computer until the time was up. Rather than being annoyed, he later cited this incident as an example of devotion to duty. Years earlier, another professor who was also made to wait a while, reported me to the police. Here we see the difference between humility and *abhiman* (pride).

Our relationship intensified when we, as joint editors, brought out the book *My Dear Master* which is the correspondence between Rabindranath Tagore and his German translator Helene Meyer-Franck (Rabindra Bhavana, Shantiniketan 1999; 2nd edition 2010). It is Prasanta da's only book in English. He also wrote a long and personal foreword to my Bengali study on Tagore's relationship with Germany, 'Germany-te Rabindra bhiksha' (translated and edited by Jaykrishna Kayal. Mitra & Ghosh, Kolkata, 1999). During those years I was deeply involved in translating Rabindranath's poems into German. I took the help of various friends to read them out to me and to explain its hidden implications and allusions. I made dozens of visits to Prasanta da's house in Aban Palli, where he lived with his family, to get his help.

He explained every line to me with their different layers of meaning and even offered his own interpretations. I then realised the hollowness of the critique that Prasanta K. Paul's scholarship was confined to being a collector of facts. He did not merely collect the facts of Rabindranath's life and coordinate them chronologically, he sifted and weighed them, put them into perspective and applied a preliminary comment or interpretation. His nine volumes of *Rabijibani* will be the foundation for future generations of Tagore scholarship. He knew the importance of his life's work, and that knowledge, I believe, kept him going.

Unfortunately, he was not well accepted by the Shantiniketan establishment. True, Prasanta da had his rough edges and could be blunt at times which may have hurt several egos. But why, I ask, could one not accommodate the idiosyncrasies of a scholar of such unique merit? How many in his generation have done as much for making Tagore known to his own people as he has? When he suffered a bad stroke and it became gradually apparent that he would be unable to complete the tenth volume, it would have been such a gracious gesture to bestow an honour on him. Even the Rabindra Puraskar of the West Bengal Government came late in his life, and I remember his childlike joy when he announced it to me.

His illness was a horrible burden on him. He sat endlessly in his small room, surrounded by shelves of books, by computers and a television and other electronic devices. 'Are you making any progress?' I would ask. And he invariably shook his head, 'Just a few lines'. As he felt depressed, he became more and more lonely. In the last few years he had hardly any visitors and almost no encouragement from outside his family.

I like to remember Prasanta da sitting on his specially designed 'three-wheeler' which was a motorbike with two wheels fitted in the rear. He suffered from gout and was of stout stature, which restricted his mobility. The two wheels in the back made it easy for him to climb his vehicle and start off. I enjoy remembering him as a techno-savvy man who was clever with computers and electronics which contrasted ingeniously with his old-world charm. Especially I want to remember him as a man who had found his life's work by doggedly writing one volume of Tagore's life after another. I consider him blessed for having discovered what he was born for early in life. On every Bengali New Year and on my birthdays, I used to visit Prasanta da in the morning and offer my *pranam* to him. Prasanta Kumar Paul died on 26 November 2007.

Birth Centenary of Moni Moulik

When I arrived at Shantiniketan in December 1979, I first found a room in the house of Dr Nag in the Ratan Palli market area. Soon I discovered that the din and bustle of the market was too much to bear. After two weeks I opted to move away and asked Prof Kalidas Bhattacharya, whether he had any suggestion for a better place. The renowned philosopher and former Vice-Chancellor of Visva-Bharati had accepted me as his doctoral student, and we had been able to develop a close understanding from the beginning. 'Kalidas da' sent me to the house of Dr Moni Moulik with a letter. Kalidas da and Dr Moulik knew each other well enough for Kalidas da to request him to put me up in a room. And Dr Moulik respected Kalidas Bhattacharya well enough to immediately agree.

There are two outhouses on the compound of 'Madhusree', one in each corner: one with a large room, a kitchen and attached bathroom, and the other with a small room and a bathroom. The larger outhouse was then occupied by an American lady professor for a year. Although Dr Moulik did not find the smaller room suitable for tenants and normally did not rent it out, he offered it to me spontaneously. I was totally pleased with this arrangement. The size of the room did not matter I was more concerned about having a peaceful, natural environment. And that, indeed, I had in plenty at Madhusree. The lush garden with its trees and bushes and flowers and the peace that reigned around me made it possible for me to begin my life at Shantiniketan.

Moni Moulik was an ideal mentor. He represented a splendid mixture of Indian and western culture and lifestyle. He was the Italian *senatore* as much as the Bengali *bhadralok*. Deeply rooted in Bengali life–probably more deeply than he cared to admit–he resided on the upper floor of his palatial house with the dignity of a *jamidar* (zamindar) of the old, genteel and noble kind. This upper floor was very much his small kingdom into which few dared to intrude. Anybody wanting to come up, be it the *dhobi* or any guest, had first to pass the scrutiny of his *thakur*, the faithful cook, who occupied the lower realms. Then the *thakur* would call up and only after Moni Moulik advanced to the railing of the upper verandah and nodded consent, would the guest be let upstairs.

Many a time, I saw him from the garden having his meal on the verandah, or reading a book, or just musing. Many a time, I was invited up to join him for tea. Our conversations were always meaningful. He dipped deep into his life experiences telling not only about his stays in Japan, in the US, and particularly in Rome, but he also shared his insights into Japanese, American and Italian culture. He was jovial, fatherly and affectionate with me. I believe, with me he was more a European talking to a fellow European. That is why, I never came to call him 'Moni da' in Shantiniketan fashion, but in European style he always was 'Mr Moulik' for me.

As we became closer, he began to invite me to have 'pot luck' and share his lunch. After a while, Mr Moulik had me over for lunch every day. This relieved me of the duty to buy and prepare food for myself, something I regularly forgot until my hungry stomach interfered. These lunches were the time to inform each other of the daily goings-on, of little satisfactions or disappointments, of the book Mr Moulik was reading, of my progress with learning Bengali and working on my thesis.

He introduced me to several distinguished persons of the Shantiniketan ashram who otherwise I may not have met. I particularly remember Mr Moulik introducing me to Leela Mazumdar, the writer of children's literature, and her husband. Oh, the affection, Leela di poured on me! I often visited them, with or without Mr Moulik, for their evening *adda* in their garden at Ratan Palli. He also introduced me to the then Vice-Chancellor, Prof. Surajit Sinha, and he wrote about my translation of the *Kathamrita* in *The Statesman* giving me my first ever exposure to the Bengali public.

At critical moments, Mr Moulik was present to give me emotional support which I, a newcomer and single like him, needed. I remember the day when the telegram informing me of my father's death reached me, he called me upstairs and affectionately listened to my childhood stories.

Yet, Mr Moulik never interfered with my life, like checking on my visitors or monitoring my activities as can be the obsession of certain landlords. All he wanted was security. The garden gate had to be locked by 10 pm. Obscure characters were not welcomed into the compound. For the rest, I had all the freedom I needed.

Moni Moulik shared with me his more hidden passions, music and poetry. He loved western classical music. His record player and his sound-boxes were excellent for that time, and he often would sit on the eastern end of his verandah, smoke and listen to music in silence. Often, he called me up when he had completed a new poem, and read it out with so much emotion that he was close to shedding tears. He was a deeply emotional man. Alas, he had few occasions in those last years of his life to vent these emotions or find solace in regular conversations with like-minded people of his own age group. There were his friends from the senior citizens' group called 'Albola'. But who else? It was not difficult to notice that he was lonely. The interminable power cuts, the heat, the dust perturbed him; he felt fretful especially when he had to sit in the dark with a candle before him with swarms of mosquitoes swirling around him. At times like that I would hear him say: 'Oh, why did I not stay on in Italy where I could have led a more enjoyable life?' He had returned to India for his wife's sake. After she had died a premature death, he could no longer start life all over again by moving back to Rome.

In his best moments, Moni Moulik was filled with mirth and wonder about nature around him. In Shantiniketan he was able to admire nature more than he ever could have in Rome. Then he wrote lovely poetry about his communion with trees and flowers and declared that the 'mystic bug' had 'bit' him. Then he was content to be álone and be in Shantiniketan, and he would just sit and muse...

I stayed on at 'Madhusree' for eleven years. After the American professor had left, Mr Moulik urged me to shift to the larger outhouse. When it could no longer contain my books and research material, I moved to a two-room bungalow three-hundred yards away where I still live. However, by the time I moved out, Moni Moulik was no longer alive.

During the last one year or one-and-a-half years of his life he was getting frail and weak and stayed in Bangalore with his elder daughter, Achala. I had met his two daughters who rather frequently came on visits to Shantiniketan. I am so pleased that we kept up a cordial relationship even after their father passed away on 7 February 1990, and after I had moved away. Whenever Aloka di and her husband come to 'Madhusree' I visit them and sit with them on that eastern side of the upper verandah. And quite frequently our conversations turn to her father and about the time when I would sit with him on that very same spot and talk about life and its concerns.

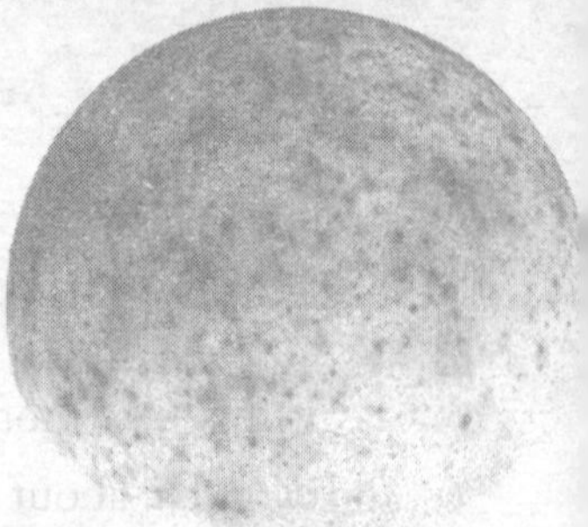

The Rabindra Mela in New Jersey

[When I was invited to participate in the third Rabindra Mela, a Tagore festival held at Ewing in New Jersey, some two hours from Manhattan and a few miles from Princeton University in 2003, I took the opportunity to look around and meet friends. These were my observations.]

As a student I spent one year at an American high school. Later I had returned to the US to explore the country. But my studies complete, I left straight for India to teach in Kolkata, and I did not return to the US for thirty-five years. In Madras, now Chennai, I launched a second course of studies and finally settled at Shantiniketan in order to write and translate. Anxious to establish myself in my profession, I gave myself no time to travel to distant countries thereafter. My life centred on the Indian subcontinent and my work. At the most, I shuttled between India and Germany if and when necessary. So when I received the invitation to the US, I wondered whether it was a welcome sign or a distraction. I took it as a welcome: It was perhaps time to extend the axis India-Germany and widen my horizon. My visit to America nonetheless revolved around my Indian experience. I wanted to meet Indians and Bangladeshis in America to discover the fabled 'non-resident Indians' and understand how they lived.

Even before the Mela, the first opportunity for such an interaction happened with the Bangladeshi writer and scholar, Farida Majid, who lived all by herself in a large flat in uptown Manhattan, an area mostly inhabited by Caribbean immigrants. She taught English, wrote on Rabindranath and participated in all forums that encouraged dialogue between eastern and western cultures. She mentioned, at that time, that there were nine Bengali weeklies published from the American East Coast, and three Bengali television channels kept the Bengalis amused. She also told me about the 'Bishsho Shahitto Kendro', a non-profit arts organisation, founded by Bangladeshi Americans, which had a very active New York branch. I was astonished, to say the least.

I was told how the Kendro, together with the local government and the Queens Council on the Arts, organised a 'South Asia Arts Day' recently, with poetry readings and panel discussions on art and music of the South Asian diaspora in Queens, a Ghazal performance, Rabindra Sangeet and of course Bengali cuisine. The event was organised at Jackson Heights in Queens which is one of the suburban districts of New York. The Kendro's yearbook also proved how many Bangladeshi writers, scholars and journalists were active in the New York area. Farida told me that the Bangladeshi community was culturally much more enterprising than the immigrants of West Bengal. Why would this be so, I wondered. Maybe because the Bangladeshi community was comparatively small and needed to be active in order to be noticed? Maybe because the Bengali language had a special significance in Bangladesh as the state was the result of a struggle to speak the mother tongue?

Later at her favourite Caribbean restaurant Farida pointed out that though it may be considered unusual for intellectuals of the subcontinent to live among Hispanics, in the US Bangladeshis, Indians and Pakistanis forgot their political and religious differences and moved together. But as much as the peoples of the Indian subcontinent stuck together abroad, they tended—Farida said—to adopt a condescending attitude towards Afro-Americans and Hispanic Americans. I was, unfortunately, able to verify this remark on several occasions.

To my surprise and joy I also discovered an 'American Shantiniketan' only a few miles away from the venue of the Rabindra Mela. This was the sprawling campus of Princeton University with its lush green lawns and unpretentious houses generously spaced over a large area. None of the atmosphere of the mass education culture, which Rabindranath zealously avoided at Shantiniketan, none of the city arrogance, could be noticed in the architecture and in the environment. Princeton looks like a dignified, modest rural University campus of the kind Tagore would have appreciated. When I paid a visit to the German literature professor, Walter Hinderer, I entered one of these beautiful old-style cottages with low ceilings and dark wood-panelling, which reminded me distinctly of the colonial houses Rabindranath had encountered in India. Incidentally, Princeton was the immigrant home of Albert Einstein who met Rabindranath in Berlin and in New York, four times in 1926 and 1930.

October 2003 saw several hundred families from West Bengal and a few from Bangladesh arrive from all over the American East Coast to attend the Rabindra Mela—to listen to Rabindra Sangeet, to watch dance dramas and plays and most of all to renew friendship with Bengali food and enjoy hours of *adda*.

The driving force behind this third Rabindra Mela was Banani Ghosh, who for decades had been teaching Rabindra Sangeet throughout the US. She seemed to me a passionate ambassador of Rabindra Sangeet, flying off every weekend to different cities to teach her students and thus keeping the flame of Rabindranath's sentiments alive across the country.

The show had been inaugurated by Nabaneeta Dev Sen, a famous Bengali author, and thereafter the audience was treated to two days of uninterrupted performances right into the night. There was a lively get-together in the large community hall, similar to an all-night performance of classical music. Parallel to this, lectures were being delivered in a smaller hall.

I have met many families from the Indian subcontinent in my native Germany. They are, typically, engineers and technicians, businessmen and doctors, like their relatives in the US. Most of them arrived in Germany as students, met German girls, married and settled in Germany. Only a minority went home to bring back newly-wed wives through arranged marriages. With a German spouse, integration into the social fabric of the host country was much easier but the number of immigrants was too small to form neighbourhoods like the ones in the US. Bangladeshis and Indians who eventually integrated into German society did so with some difficulty at times. Above all, they had to adopt the rhythm of a German life with its sparing, less emotional social contacts, and make the best of it. The second generation, however, had totally adapted to the European way of life often feeling little allegiance to their parents' home.

In the US the situation was different. At the Rabindra Mela I did not meet a single 'mixed' couple. All Bengali men had Bengali wives. On enquiry, I learnt that the majority of men and women had arrived in the US as young professionals and not as students. They had spent considerably more time in their homeland, absorbing its cultural system, than their counterparts in Europe, thus bringing with them stronger cultural ties.

I was the only non-Bengali participant apart from the American artist, Mark W. McGinnis, who arrived with 103 small-sized paintings each inspired by one of the texts of the English *Gitanjali*. And there was the endearing German artist-philosopher, Andor Orand Carius, a close friend of the Bengali community, who read out a conversation Rabindranath Tagore had with Albert Einstein, and then spoke expressively on the relevance of this conversation for a better understanding of 'East' and 'West'.

I was astonished to realise how large the number of singers and dancers was that had arrived from various corners of the US for the occasion. Their expertise was no less than the groups in India which put up performances at large neighbourhood clubs; their enthusiasm was perhaps more soulful, enhanced perhaps by the distance from the homeland and their feeling of isolation. Surprisingly, these groups consisted of the young second-generation Indians born in the US who spoke in fluent Bengali, albeit with a slight American drawl, but seemed to have fully imbibed the Rabindric idiom. This goes to show how anxious immigrant parents are for their children to maintain their cultural legacy.

I share the fate of non-resident Indians, having left my native home Germany in my twenties to spend my professional life in India—though my reasons may have been quite different from those Indians and Bangladeshis staying in America. Living in one's native country has certain advantages when it comes to generating mental and emotional energy that comes from the stability of being rooted, but the tensions and frictions of a life away from home are fruitful as well. In our second home we are, even after twenty or thirty years of residence, still testing the parameters of society, probing what makes people tick, never shaking off the slight insecurity—our understanding of our country of adoption being not by instinct, but by a laborious and continuous process of acquisition.

We may regret this predicament of 'never fully belonging', and weak minds may succumb to a sense of alienation. In our best moments, however, we realise that this situation, of participating in two societies and cultures, harbours an enormous potential for creativity. This creativity can flow into works of art, into music and literature. It may also manifest itself in a lifestyle which brings out the best of our native culture combined with valuable and necessary traits of our country of adoption.

While in the US, I met two Indians who have achieved this aim admirably. After many years I again saw Samir Chatterjee, a tabla player, who was my student in German class in the 1970s in Kolkata. We had maintained a close contact ever since. He had been employed by All India Radio in Cuttack and Kolkata, all along making a name for himself as a consummate tabla accompanist and tabla teacher. He was already in his early forties when he with his family shifted base to the American East Coast.

After arriving in New York, I visited his home across the Hudson River in suburban New Jersey. Within a decade he had established himself as a leading tabla player. He told me that almost every weekend he flew off to concerts in different places in North America. During the week he taught individual students among who were also young American musicians. Samir loved to play the tabla for Fusion Jazz. He had bought a house for his family and was comfortably settled. Both, success and professional fulfilment were evident. But more than anything else his reach to the American public at large, making his Indian cultural sentiments relevant to others, was commendable.

He took me to Jackson Heights which was almost exclusively inhabited by people of the Indian subcontinent. We saw advertisements written in Bengali in Bangladeshi shops. We could buy spices, tropical fruits, saris, ornaments for weddings, anything pertaining to the traditional subcontinental way of life. The lanes were neat, overflowing with well-dressed, busy people. The area exuded a nonchalant confidence, reminiscent of the lanes in Dhaka and Kolkata.

The second person was Nupur Lahiri, a doctor and psychiatrist who lead a busy life serving the American public with her knowledge. I was told she was careful about accepting patients from the subcontinent as she was emotionally too close to them to have the objective distance needed to provide psychological help. Her son was an actor at London's West End. With all her success, she had started the 'Bengal Foundation' and in her spacious house she organised numerous events of music, poetry reading and lectures meant for an American audience. Nupur was also a singer with a CD of Bengali songs to her credit. It was people like Samir and Nupur who seemed to infuse fresh life into the new world they inhabited, deftly weaving new thoughts into the warp of Indian traditions.

Reflecting on my experiences with the Indian and Bangladeshi Americans in New York and New Jersey, I realised the need for a home in *one* place, for *one* nourishing earth where one's roots are deep, since it was not possible to live fully in both cultures. Whoever keeps these roots intact, can live on in a second country with a positive attitude.

Rabindranath Tagore's Global Reach

[This is the abridged version of the Convocation Address delivered at Rabindra-Bharati University, Kolkata, in 2012.]

I want to share the one emotion that overwhelms me while I stand before you. That is: how enormously fortunate you are—all of you before me who know Bengali as their mother tongue—to have grown up speaking, reading and writing the language which Rabindranath Tagore used. The blessing you have received by being at home in Bengali as your mother-tongue cannot be overestimated. I began learning Bengali at Shantiniketan when I had already crossed thirty. I wanted to read the *Kathamrita* and Rabindranath's poems. For several years I made a sincere effort to learn Bengali as perfectly as possible—to enter into the depth of Rabindranath's emotions and his subconsciousness. All I can say is that I am still learning even after spending several decades at Shantiniketan and using the language every day. Nothing can compensate for that blessing of being born to know Rabindranath's language. Each time I return from abroad and enter Kolkata and its language again, I feel so humble realising that I am and will continue to be a learner.

Please remember, Rabindranath Tagore, the great classic writer of Bengali language and literature, is your contemporary. He has experienced in his lifetime many of the important transformations that have resulted in our modern age in India. He saw the beginning of industrialisation and portrayed it in plays like *Mukta dhara* and *Raktakarabi*. He experienced urbanisation, population explosion, the beginning of a movement towards greater freedom for women, towards the freedom from caste sentiments, towards universal education, towards a democratisation of society with greater justice for marginalised groups. Rabindranath already spoke, wrote and fought for these issues which are still so topical today.

Having realised this, turn to the classical writers of other countries: William Shakespeare lived in the 16th and early 17th century; Victor Hugo and Charles Baudelaire of France in the 19th century; Dante of Italy even earlier, in the 13th and 14th century; and Germany's Goethe lived in the 18th and early 19th century. None of them has shared the 20th century with us, witnessed modernity and become part of our contemporary consciousness. None of them can directly guide us in our modern dilemmas and confusions–except Rabindranath Tagore.

The grace of a birth inside Rabindranth's charmed circle does not, however, come without its challenges and responsibilities. It is important to question how true we have been to the core concerns of the Poet. Rabindranath wanted, for himself, for his children and for his society, an education which was unfettered by the kind of 'achievement' and 'success' which can be measured in numbers and given expression through examinations. He wanted an education which was creative, which not only informed and helped to acquire knowledge, but also inspired and built character. Looking at our present education in India we have to humbly admit we have failed our Poet. The boys and girls in our villages and towns continue to memorise their lessons and strive for little more than 'numbers'. The term 'by hearting' is particularly cruel because it has nothing to do with the heart. We may argue that the kind of education Rabindranath wanted can be afforded only by privileged children who need not struggle for jobs and a livelihood. But when these privileged ones aim to become doctors, engineers, government employees, financers and businessmen and have no craving for a wider fulfilment, then they too forfeit the greater vision of the Poet.

Rabindra-Bharati is the university which needs to be the trailblazer for advocating a greater balance between the demands of the job market and the natural creative instincts. It must demonstrate that a proficiency in literature and the arts and an enthusiasm for creative activity can indeed lead to remunerative professions. If we as Bengalis and Bengali-speaking people enjoy the privilege of having Rabindranath Tagore as our guide, then we must feel urged to rethink our educational targets. We can easily create some areas of education in every school and college which are obligatory but kept outside the purview of examinations.

My faith in this kind of education prompted me to help start and support a non-formal Santal school, the Rolf Schoembs Vidyashram, eight kilometres from Shantiniketan, established by educated Santals. It combines the need to instil knowledge with a child's desire for play, song, dance, for art and creative interaction. It is now being recognised a model institution.

The second challenge and responsibility would be to emulate Rabindranath as an *activist*. What do I mean by this? Our radio programmes and television channels perform Rabindra Sangeet every day and sometimes several hours per day. This is indeed welcome as Tagore's songs can mould our emotions and strengthen our moral fibre; they can make us more sensitive human beings. Our schools, youth clubs and theatre groups perform Tagore's plays; we enjoy recitation competitions declaiming Tagore poems with passionate abandon. Indeed, we value Tagore the poet, the composer, the playwright and the author of novels and stories. Yet, we largely ignore the Tagore who reached out to the neighbouring villages with his rural reconstruction programmes. We know of Rabindranath's love and pity for the village leaseholders on the East Bengal family estate. He poured out this love not only in his famous stories, but also in practical social work among his villagers. When Rabindranath settled in Shantiniketan, he almost immediately founded his village work in neighbouring Sriniketan. For him it was quite unthinkable to build an ideal school with a few children mostly recruited from Kolkata while around him in the villages people lived in poverty and ignorance. Idealism can never see things in isolation.

By force of his moral sensitivity, Rabindranath became a social activist working patiently for the education, the human rights, the good health, the self-confidence of the village population. Following him on that path is more difficult than singing *ekla cholo re* and reciting his poems. But if we are serious in loving and appreciating Rabindranath, as we so often profess, we cannot avoid following him in his social action as well, even though it may be a lonely path.

May 2012 saw the conclusion of a grand year celebrating the 150th year of Rabindranath's birth. The Indian government supported the commemorative efforts with generous funds—but money alone could not generate the genuine and innovative interest that was witnessed in many countries in the preceding twelve months. Numerous anthologies and special journals came out and some are yet to appear. More and more professional translations of Tagore's poetry and prose and plays are about to be published. The largest potential for innovation lies in the performance of Tagore's songs and plays, his musical dramas, and poetry. In them, Rabindranath's ideas and visions can always be found echoing the contemporary needs and tastes without falsifying his original creative impulse.

The stage is the place where Rabindranath's images and narratives most easily enwrap the viewer with their magic. There have been many such efforts, especially outside and inside India. The stage can comfortably offer opportunities of intercultural experiments and expressions. For example, a German music composer recently used Rabindra Sangeet as his inspiration and created a long piece for a German choir.

The choir members sang some Bengali words as well as a few lines in German, like mantras, while slowly encircling the entire audience. Listening to the same words from all sides, the audience lived within a sound-space which gradually elevated them into a separate sphere of rapture. What can be more Rabindric than creating such an atmosphere?

Elevation into a sphere of rapture was what European, especially German, audiences have been expecting all along from Rabindranath. In Germany, the Indian poet was not the subject of a colonised country, he was not a representative of a country that was to be economically exploited. Rather, in Germany, Tagore was what he essentially was: a romantic poet. He fell in line with the German tradition of Romanticism which had begun in the early 19th century. It was no coincidence that it was the same time German scholars 'discovered' their interest in India and began to study her philosophy and mythology. Indian culture continued to be associated with Romanticism in Germany, and Rabindranath was the final great figure in whom German Romanticism and India united. Did Rabindranath not himself imagine that he was a romantic writer, ever yearning for the 'far away', for an unknowable 'beyond'?

This affinity between German Romanticism with Rabindranath had become obvious from the moment Rabindranath set foot on German soil in 1921. After the Second World War, the German people were especially vulnerable. They had lost the war, lost many young men in its battles; they had sunk into an emotional and cultural crisis.

Rabindranath arrived like a saviour and relished this role which was a decidedly romantic one. We do not know what exactly Rabindranath had read of German Romanticism, except Heine, or of the country's classical literature, except Goethe's drama *Faust*. But we do know that he felt a deep attraction to the German romantic spirit as he mentioned it again and again.

Asked why I continue my life in India for the last almost forty years, staying at Shantiniketan and writing on India, I come–being totally true to myself–to the same conclusion: because of this romantic sweep of emotionality, that carries one upward and gives one that rapture which Rabindranath evoked in his finest poems. Translating his works, and thus communing with the *jiban-debata* in his poems, have been some of my happiest moments.

In Europe, romantic feelings are looked upon nowadays with a certain scepticism. The last World War was fought with a surfeit of passion and ended in disaster. Any excess of emotions is dangerous. Therefore many intellectuals in the West have kept a distance from Rabindranath. They did not know the whole of him and his work. How could they? Rabindranath himself preferred to present his romantic side to the West.

Now the time has come to work towards an image of Rabindranath Tagore which encompasses his entire humanity and the whole gamut of his work. Let us say farewell to the old man with the long beard and the Sufi cap and see the complementing and conflicting strands of Rabindranath's character and work as well. He himself confessed to his restlessness, his continuous yearning for and discovery of new 'material' with which to fire one's creativity: new sense-impressions, novel emotions, encounters with new people. We cannot tie down the Poet to his meditative moods. In order to discover Rabindranath's fullness, we ourselves must grow.

Hermann Keyserling and his School of Wisdom

[In 2003, I had the opportunity to visit the Estonian capital, Tallinn (former Reval), when I was invited to a conference to speak on philosopher and writer Hermann Keyserling, who in 1912 had visited Rabindranath Tagore's family in Kolkata.]

Before the iron curtain crashed down over a decade ago and Soviet Union became history, we in Central Europe had practically no opportunity to visit the three small Baltic states of Estonia, Latvia and Lithuania. We hardly knew their names and were not really aware that these three countries clustering around the Baltic Sea had a sizable German-speaking population—the so-called Baltic Germans, who enjoyed a privileged status in society.

Until the Russian Revolution, they were the landed gentry with large estates to their name. One of these German-speaking aristocratic families, living in Estonia since generations, was the Keyserling family. Of them, three great intellectuals made their mark and are still known as personalities of historical importance. They are Alexander Keyserling (1815–1891) who was a renowned geologist and palaeontologist; Eduard von Keyserling (1855–1918), a fiction writer and playwright; and

Hermann Keyserling (1880–946), the cultural philosopher.

Estonia turned into a democratic republic with an elected parliament during the years 1988 to 1991. The population was more than happy to break loose from an unloved Soviet embrace. Enormous energies were set free, and within a span of fifteen years, Estonia's economic life had progressed dramatically. The population resolutely veered from looking at the Soviet East to latching on to the West European market economy. In 2004, Estonia voted to become a member of the European Union.

My subject during the conference, was to probe into the relationship between the Baltic count, Hermann Keyserling, and the Bengal poet, Rabindranath Tagore. The conference was held in German language for the general public which shows that German was still alive in a section of the population, although of course the feudal Baltic lords were gone.

Hermann Keyserling had left his family estate Rayküll to study at nearby Dorpat. Then he moved on to live in different west European countries, returning to Rayküll occasionally and finally settled in Darmstadt, a medium-sized town south of Frankfurt. This was in 1920. Hermann Keyserling and his entire family had been dispossessed in 1917 during the Russian Revolution and had fled their country. Keyserling was given shelter by the Archduke Ernst Ludwig of Hesse who himself had been dispossessed and lost his power as a consequence of the First World War.

Ernst Ludwig, a patron of the arts, appreciated Keyserling's idea of starting a 'School of Wisdom', a kind of academy which would train promising men and women to become 'wise', cultivated human beings. They were to assist in the reconstruction of German culture after the deep crisis the German people slid into, following the defeat in the First World War. Until the dawn of Hitler's Third Reich, Keyserling lead this school and organised numerous seminars for the general public and more exclusive study sessions. The first such seminar was the so-called 'Tagore Week' in June 1921 when Rabindranath visited Darmstadt and held daily public lectures.

This was the culmination of a development which began in 1911 when Hermann Keyserling set sail in Italy to travel around the world. He voyaged through the Suez Canal to Ceylon where he began his exploration of the Indian subcontinent. He travelled to Rameswaram, Ellora, to Delhi and west to Lahore, then east to Varanasi and finally to Calcutta where he 'discovered' Rabindranath as a spiritual genius. He wrote, 'Rabindranath, the poet, impressed me like a guest from a higher, more spiritual world. Never perhaps have I seen so much spiritualised substance of soul condensed into one man.' You find these lines in Hermann Keyserling's best-known book, *The Travel Diary of a Philosopher* (1918), which is still being read. Published immediately after the First World War, it became one of the most influential books of its time.

After Rabindranath was awarded the Nobel Prize, the entire world began to honour him. Keyserling was, however, among those few who sensed his genius earlier. He began his correspondence with Tagore several months before the Nobel Prize, offering his assistance to Tagore who had planned a trip to Germany and Italy. After the Nobel Prize was announced, Keyserling generously wrote to Tagore: 'I have been very glad that the Nobel Prize has been awarded to you. Not indeed for your sake–you are beyond prizes and praises–but for the sake of India.'

Keyserling planned to visit India again, but the war stopped him. When Tagore expressed his intention to visit Germany, Keyserling immediately extended his invitation. Keyserling suggested that, rather than travelling throughout Germany to meet like-minded people, Tagore make his centre at Darmstadt and ask all intellectuals to flock there. The Baltic count was an imperious, overbearing personality, gushingly eloquent, quick-witted and endowed with a mighty appetite for life. Clearly, he wanted to monopolise the Indian poet and get the credit for having presented him to the German public first. It would have given Keyserling's School of Wisdom the kick-off it needed.

Rabindranath sensed this danger and wrote a mildly indignant letter: '... It will be wrong for me to be narrowly exclusive in my selection of place, parties or friends.' He further mentioned that the press notice Keyserling was about to release 'should have nothing in it in its reference to me which would make me blush or make it appear that I identify myself with only one institution in this country...' The result was that Count Keyserling organised the 'Tagore Week' (10–14 June 1921) in Darmstadt during which the poet gave several informal public lectures per day at the Archduke's palatial home. Keyserling translated them directly. It was a resounding success and a historical event which is still being written about.

The two men never met again, although Rabindranath visited Germany twice thereafter, in 1926 and 1930. Keyserling continued to speak highly, indeed, superlatively, of Tagore. On the occasion of Tagore's seventieth birthday (1931), Keyserling wrote: 'Rabindranath Tagore is the greatest man I have had the privilege to know...There has been no one like him anywhere on our globe for many and many centuries.' Elsewhere he pronounced: 'Tagore is without doubt one of the highest expressions of the Indian genius of all time.' Keyserling yearned for the 'new man', or 'ecumenical man', 'the wise one' after whom he hoped to fashion his School of Wisdom. Presumably he meant a person who had succeeded in unfolding his entire human potential and thus had become broad-minded, endowed with an all-encompassing sympathy and understanding. Both persons were driven by an enormous sense of mission.

The success of the 'Travel Diary' encouraged Keyserling into believing that he was the intellectual mouthpiece of his epoch in the West. Similarly, after the Nobel Prize, Rabindranath regarded himself as the voice not only of the Indian subcontinent, but of 'the East'. The professed aim of both men was to bring about a synthesis of 'East' and 'West'; they proclaimed its urgent need from numerous platforms. Rabindranath felt the necessity to assimilate the good qualities of the West to enrich India and Asia. Conversely, Keyserling saw in the East the key to revitalise western culture after the war. With these aims in mind, both men established non-formal schools. Rabindranath founded Visva-Bharati in

December 1921, immediately after returning from Europe, while Hermann Keyserling had already founded the School of Wisdom a year earlier. Although dissimilar in character and temperament, Tagore and Keyserling pursued much the same ideas and ideals.

The correspondence between the poet and the count continued until 1938. Meanwhile, Keyserling got several essays of his published in Tagore's journal *Visva-Bharati Quarterly*. Yet, in a number of his letters to Tagore he complained irascibly about not getting his due and being misunderstood. The only response Keyserling got was a sharply critical review by Surendranath Tagore of his book *The Art of Life* .

Hermann Keyserling's School of Wisdom had to fold up under pressure from the Nazis. He became a critic of the Third Reich and was forbidden to speak and publish. He showed immense courage by publicly speaking out against the Nazi Fascists, and only his high aristocratic status and his social connections saved him from imprisonment. Soon after the war, Hermann Keyserling died in Austria, a disgruntled and disappointed man. His hopes to revive the School of Wisdom could not be realised.

At the seminar in the city of Tartu in Estonia, I was attending in 2003, several members of the Keyserling family joined. They had arrived from the US, Canada and Germany. Several spoke German haltingly and with an accent. None of them, I believe, had ever visited Estonia, the country of their forefathers. With deep emotions they listened to the deliberations of us academicians on the achievements of their three famous family members. One of the Keyserlings finally stood up and confessed: 'I have lived in the US most of my life. I have succeeded in my profession, but I have never been quite at home there. Coming here to Estonia for the first time, I realise that you give me back my home and my family. My parents told us many sad stories about war crimes and about refugees, lost homes, scattered families, deported relatives. These stories were so depressing that we never really wanted to see the countries of east Europe where all this had happened. Now that we have finally arrived here I realise that this visit and this conference initiate for us a process of healing.'

Tallinn, the capital, is a city reverberating with vitality. It is a port-town opening up to Finland and Russia. The ferry boat to Helsinki takes three hours to cross. With a population of just four lakhs, Tallinn is small by Indian standard. Before landing I saw the drab suburbs which we associate with the housing of socialist countries. But as I walked around the old centre of the town, I discovered its excitingly picturesque architecture representing a variety of historical styles. Some buildings were still dilapidated but the majority of them had been delicately restored and repainted–and all this in less than fifteen years! I was surprised by the bubbling nightlife with groups of young people milling around in the streets. There were an ample number of discotheques and clubs, restaurants and bistros. I discovered an active cultural life with, of course, the University, the Estonian National Opera, the Art Museum, the National Library, the Music Academy, and the Arts Academy. The newspaper listed about ten theatres which offered performances, and many more cinemas. These youthful crowds were exuberant, however not bawdy or disorderly. Although older to them by one generation, I felt comfortable in their midst. At the Tallinn market place it was warm enough to sit outside in the evening and watch the activity on the old square covered with lovely cobble stones. Like most churches and historical buildings the square was illuminated. I absorbed the energy of the people who blended with the lights and shadows of the historical square.

All participants of the conference took a bus to Rayküll to visit the Keyserling estate. It was a lovely ride. The Estonian countryside was sparsely populated. We were told that the shift of the economic model from socialist collective to private ownership of the fields takes time to be entirely profitable. Still many fields were fallow. Immense wooded areas! We saw nothing but forests, fields and meadows for two hours. The forest trees already wore the red-yellow glow of autumn. In this inclement northerly climate, the summers are short and the frosty winters spread out for three or four long months. So the autumns arrive earlier than, say, in Germany. I love the melancholy colours of this season, and regret on my home visits to Germany that I must return to India before I can see the fullness of autumn. This year, Estonia has given me the gift of its brilliant autumn hues.

Visiting the Keyserling estate stirred mixed feelings in us. Left intact were the venerable old trees exquisitely grouped in an extensive park area. The mansion itself is a ruin, or rather a construction site. During the communist era, a home for mentally challenged children was housed in the big building. One of them set it on fire leaving a cavernous ruin. Recently, an elderly couple has bought the huge house and tried to reconstruct it. Seeing the present state, we could neither sense how it looked like when the Keyserling family dwelled in it, nor predict what it will be after restoration is complete.

While travelling I wondered whether Hermann Keyserling can be resurrected in our present time. His association with Tagore will remain important in the context of Rabindranath's life. But apart from his vibrant 'Travel Diary' will Hermann Keyserling's works and ideas still speak to us today? I am afraid not.

The Abiding Importance of Swami Vivekananda

If it were not for Swami Vivekananda, I would not have made Bengal my home and stayed on for forty years. He is my early inspiration and has been my loyal companion, especially in hard times. From him I have learnt about strength of will and the confidence never to say: 'No, I can't!'

Looking back, I remember how I began my life in Shantiniketan with a small and irregular income from writing and translating, without a long-term visa, making do in one small room, without any sponsors or friends to stand by me, suffering all the everyday inconveniences that I was not used to, especially, power cuts and the near 100 per cent humidity. And yet, I began to research for a thesis, learnt Bengali, began to translate Sri Ramakrishna's *Kathamrita* and Rabindranath Tagore's poetry, and got involved, initially against some local opposition, in the long-term development of two Santal villages. The strength came from Swami Vivekananda's furious assertion: 'Nothing is impossible!'

During the first three years in India, I had a small room in the Ramakrishna Mission Ashram of Narendrapur, south of Kolkata, and read all the eight volumes of Vivekananda's *Complete Works*. I remember how I had to get out of my room and walk up and down on the verandah to calm myself down. The spiritual stimulation induced by the Swami's words was overwhelming. What struck me was the boldness with which he invoked the spiritual dimension of life and proclaimed the supremacy of the Spirit. Was such a totally spirit-centred life possible among all our everyday struggles and preoccupations?

Swami Nikhilananda's biography and particularly his letters revealed that Vivekananda himself was, until the end of his life, struggling to align his desire to fight for human justice and spiritual liberation, and his strong inclination towards a life spent in secluded meditation, oscillating between these two strong pulls. I wondered whether he would have found a full and deeper integration of social action and contemplation had he lived thirty years longer.

Vivekananda's speeches and writings take their singular character from this tension between the active and the contemplative life. It is to his credit that he never sought and advocated easy answers to resolve this conflict. In fact, I get the impression that this internal conflict is responsible for his later-life despondency, the collapse of his health in the last few years. The lesson I draw from this is that such integration of the active and the contemplative life is the greatest challenge we face. Some saints have given emphasis to the contemplative dimension, others to the active one; yet few have, like the Swami, seen the *equal* importance of both sides.

Looking around in India, I also realise how truly modern Swami Vivekananda has been already over a century ago. His call for strength and self-reliance is the call we in Europe heard since the Age of Rationalism and Enlightenment. The individualism that sprang from it has had its benefit, but also several disastrous effects. For India, a society that has for long made a virtue out of not being individualistic but community-centred, such a call was unusual.

Here the nucleus is the family to which its members are so devoted that they can expect unstinted support and encouragement from one another. Beyond the family, support is rendered by the *para* or the village-community, by professional colleagues, by one's caste, ethnic and religious communities. All of them teach a give-and-take of support which leads to dependence rather than self-reliance, to a policy of integration, acceptance and submission rather than to developing personal reliance and strength. Here, the Swami trod a different path.

With Vivekananda, I am of the firm conviction that such family and community conventions are crucial and glorious but that they are not sufficient to master the challenges of our time. If we wish to succeed we must question and judge those conventions which may actually be regressive. Around me I continue to see young people following outdated habits and thought patterns only because their grandparents and parents demand that they adhere to them, even though they may be detrimental to the progress of society.

In such a situation, strength of action can be infused by reading Swami Vivekananda's words. I have been watching friends who had the fortitude to break out of the shell of meaningless conventions and do some work among the poor and marginalised. I so wish that Vivekananda's influence can bolster their convictions beyond the initial enthusiasm and beyond the beginning of family life which often puts a stop to such courageous endeavours.

The Ramakrishna Mission has been instrumental in spreading Swami Vivekananda's lectures and writings to the farthest corners of India. Their editions are cheap and their books well printed. The *Complete Works*, which now comprise nine volumes, can be had for the price of one or two hardcover novels. Further, several anthologies of his writings present the 'essential Vivekananda'. His life is well documented by a massive two-volume biography written anonymously by his 'eastern and western disciples' and by the indefatigable research of Marie Louise Burke whose six-volume 'Swami Vivekananda in the West' is a mine of interesting information.

Yet with all this stupendous effort that went into making Vivekananda one of the widest-read figures of modern India, the textual authenticity of his lectures and writings is by no means secure. The *Complete Works* contain a large body of very disparate texts. The lectures are strewn across various volumes, so are his writings and his letters. Even newspaper reports, on Vivekananda's lectures, find a place, mainly in the ninth volume. The impression created is one of convoluted disorder. The spelling, punctuation, diacritical marks and capitalisation have no uniformity. The text is being corrected from one edition to another without any editorial explanation. Further, the letters are reproduced with significant omissions to protect the dignity of the persons mentioned even more than a century after they were written.

We are waiting for a critical and careful edition of Vivekananda's works, similar to the editions bestowed on the works of Mahatma Gandhi and Sri Aurobindo. Further, it is regrettable that Vivekananda scholarship is still lacking in cohesion. There is, on the one side, the diligent and laudable work of the Ramakrishna Mission monks who compile and disseminate and spiritually interpret the Swami. On the other side, there are a handful of serious academicians who critically look at Vivekananda as a figure who attains significance as part of the history of the struggle for Independence, of the evolution of modern Hinduism, and of Europe's and America's discovery of India. Yet, so far, there is, very little fruitful interaction and cooperation between these two groups.

Once this happens, the stature of the Swami in the global debate will rise. His doubts and his struggles are the doubts and struggles of our modern age and that makes him a man with whom we can identify. If we see in him only a heroic, aloof figure, Vivekananda will not touch our daily lives. Despite the troubles he went through, he preached and represented unshaken strength–that makes him great!

Albert Schweitzer's Reverence for Life

Imagine this: a highly gifted man becomes an acclaimed organ-player at an early age, performs concerts in France, Spain and Germany, delivers lectures as a musicologist, and along with this he studies theology to become ordained as a pastor. He writes a brilliant thesis on the philosopher Immanuel Kant and a path-breaking book, *The Quest of the Historical Jesus*. At the age of thirty, he decides to abandon his promising career and returns to university to study medicine. Why? In order to become a physician, to live and work among remote African tribes, curing them of leprosy and other deadly diseases, and to give them a life worth living. Crazy? This is what Albert Schweitzer (1875–1965) was.

A German from the province Alsace-Lorraine, Schweitzer had decided early on that leading the life of a scholar and musician was not enough. He was convinced that our knowledge and artistic visions should flow into a life of practical engagement with the world. He therefore, renounced a self-serving life in order to serve mankind. A century ago, Albert Schweitzer rejected the fame of becoming a European scholar in order to settle in the African jungles. Albert Schweitzer continued to play the organ and write books, but these activities were now subservient to the goal of treating those men and women who had nobody to treat them.

He had completed his medical studies in February 1913, and a month later he and his wife were on their way to Lambaréné on the river Ogooué. Situated then in a French colony, it is today a town in an independent country called Gabon, West Africa. Schweitzer arrived on 16 April and began building a small hospital immediately.

When the First World War broke out, Schweitzer and his wife who were now the citizens of an enemy country were put under the supervision of the French military. In 1917, they were taken to the south of France and interned. The war over, Schweitzer's home province became a part of France, and he was free again and began raising funds by giving organ concerts. He returned to the harsh tropical climate of Lambaréné in 1924. Soon he received the help of doctors and nurses from several European countries, but his efforts to build a hospital and serve the poor and sick amounted to an extraordinarily taxing struggle against difficulties created by the ancient lifestyle of the jungle people, against famine and leprosy, and against the political elite of Africa. He did not want to turn African village people into 'modern' men and women. Rather, he pleaded that they retain their simple and natural lifestyle; critics in Europe termed this primitive and unscientific.

Ardent in his faith as a Protestant Christian, equally ardent in his belief in humanistic ideals, he never gave up. With his increasing fame, he embraced global problems; he became a harsh critic of colonialism which creates inequality and condescension. He believed that the concept of colonising was adverse to human dignity, as defined by Christian civilisation. After the Second World War, Albert Schweitzer was along with Albert Einstein, a driving force of the opposition to the nuclear bomb. The recent film *Albert Schweitzer–a Life for Africa* (2009) describes this phase of his life. He was pestered by the CIA, denounced in the US as a communist, and sabotaged by his overt and secret enemies in Lambaréné. In 1952, Schweitzer was awarded the Nobel Prize for Peace, but fame did not make his life any easier.

Schweitzer's guiding principle became 'reverence for life'. Letting his eyes wander across the Ogooué river, he in an instant perceived that 'everything that man is surrounded with –plants, animals, fellow human beings–possesses the same desire to live as we do. Whoever has understood this cannot but meet all of them with love. Respect of God who gives life to every being so that it may fulfill its responsibility, demands that we give respect to all beings and help them to fulfill themselves'.

Don't these beautiful lines echo the core the Hindu belief that all animate and inanimate entities are endowed with a soul–humans, animals, trees, water, fire, rocks and every blade of grass. Reverence for life expresses and celebrates that every being around us is a part of God's creation, infused with meaning and importance by the Creator. Therefore, don't kill! Unless totally unavoidable, don't kill even the tiniest animal. Therefore, respect and support all life! Allow life to prosper to the same extent as you yourself desire to live.

The fact that there is a food chain which preserves the balance of nature became an agonising ethical problem for Schweitzer. Animals eat other animals and plants for their survival. Natural Law and Ethical Law seem to diverge, even clash. For Schweitzer the participation in the suffering of all creatures, reminiscent of both Christian and Buddhist principles, had become important. Schweitzer seems to be more radical than most in giving expression to compassion. He wrote, 'He who has experienced within himself the misery of the world but once, can no longer become happy in the way men wish to be happy [...]. He cannot forget the poor man whom he has met, the patient whom he saw, the human being of whose sorry fate he has read...'

In another essay Schweitzer wrote, 'We live in truth when we experience the conflicts [of other creatures] more and more deeply. A good conscience is the invention of the devil.'

Yet, such radicalism did not make Albert Schweitzer a bitter zealot. Rather, he believed in a 'life-affirming' attitude. He noted, 'In no way does reverence for life allow a person to give up his interest in the world.' From his remote hospital in Africa, at a time when there was no television and no internet, this man spoke to the world and became one of its important conscience keepers. He often voyaged between Europe and

Africa and once to the US for lectures, to give organ recitals and collect funds, and he always returned to his principal mission of service.

In Lambaréné, he also studied Indian philosophy. It is a pity that he never visited India. Had he done so, his understanding of the holy scriptures would have become more complex. Schweitzer had asserted that before Rabindranath Tagore Indian philosophy was broadly guided by a 'world-and life-negating' attitude. According to him it was Rabindranath who had ushered in a fully 'world-and life-affirmating' view.

Rabindranath's response was guarded. Praising Schweitzer for his efforts to study Indian philosophy, Rabindranath (in a private letter to Schweitzer written in 1936) criticised him for not doing 'proper justice' to the Buddhist concept. 'Buddhist monks took a very active part in ministering to the cares and sufferings of the sick and the downtrodden [...].'

Albert Schweitzer and Rabindranath have a great deal in common. They were both deeply committed to the ideals of humanism and anti-nationalism. They both saw their main mission in teaching, directed to the people locally and in the world at large. Social activism, lectures, essays, philosophical books flowed from this pedagogical impulse. Rabindranath founded his school and university and attempted rural reconstruction, while Schweitzer spent a lifetime in Lambaréné. They both combined this with their creative urge. They poured out their heart in poetry, in songs and in music. They struggled to maintain a delicate balance between creative activity, scholarship and serving fellow human beings.

Since generations Albert Schweitzer has been revered as an ideal man in the West. When I was a schoolgoing boy, my father, then a college principal, wrote a letter to Albert Schweitzer requesting his support for an exhibition of his books. The great man replied with a two-page handwritten letter. After the exhibition, I kept this letter in my desk.

It was the one true treasure I harboured as an adolescent. I like to believe that my admiration for Albert Schweitzer was one of the forces that brought me to India, and his example gave me the strength to serve among people in my modest way. In 2013 and 2014, Albert Schweitzer's arrival in Lambaréné a hundred years earlier was remembered and celebrated throughout Germany and France. Few in India know about this great man and his connection to India.

Ibuki and Rabindranath's Transformative Powers

A long email arrived from a person in Germany who calls himself Ibuki. The mail recounted his entire life story. Since many years he has been a night guard in a psychiatric clinic. Originally however, his father expected him to learn the violin and dedicate himself to music. The reason was that as a young man his father had, after the Second World War, spent seven years in internment camps and returned home a severely traumatised man. The one thing which afforded him some relief was playing the violin. But Ibuki studied Social Work instead of music and followed his hobby of target-shooting.

A few years later, he renounced his hobby, sold his rifles and decided to take time off to work in Kolkata as an art dealer selling modern Indian art to European customers. This was not easy and he gave it up after some time. But he got to know his future British wife in Kolkata. She worked as a volunteer nurse in Mother Teresa's asylum for the dying. When he married and returned with his wife, Ibuki found himself a job as night guard in a psychiatric clinic. In the quiet hours of the night he learned to play the guitar. The better he mastered the instrument the happier he became because he realised how deeply attracted the psychiatric patients became to his music.

Ibuki writes that he witnessed a noticeable change in them. They became more peaceful, less tense–the atmosphere in the clinic transformed. He belatedly began to fulfil the dreams of his father who had meanwhile expired. Easing suffering through music! However, the clinic's administration saw a problem. Would the guard remain alert to any problems that may occur during his night shift if he was busy playing? Was it his task to impart occupational therapy? A general ban on music during the night was therefore enforced.

What did Ibuki do? He writes that he 'went underground', continuing to play secretly, at the risk of being dismissed. His patients kept the secret; he played the guitar for his own solace and that of a small circle of inmates. This continued for seven years. Thereafter the burden of secrecy proved to be too heavy, and Ibuki wrote a long letter to the administration which finally allowed him to play his music openly. This permission must have been given grudgingly because some time later, he was shifted away from night duty.

What makes this story remarkable for us in India? Ibuki writes that for many years a short poem by Rabindranath Tagore–translated in German–consoled him and gave him the strength to continue. The English prose translation of the four-liner is:

'The mountain must carry the weight of its snow all alone; but when it melts, it flows down and the whole world receives it with joy.'

The mountain—that is Ibuki himself. The heavy snow? That is his father's war trauma; it is also the many lonely and secret hours of unauthorised guitar play weighing him down. When would the sun arrive to melt the heaviness on his shoulders? Ibuki knew that the sun would rise one day and when it did its energy would transform whatever is oppressive into something which gifts life to the entire world. He concludes his letter: 'My story can result in something for the world at large, if only we add our creative energy to it.' He means that in itself his story is commonplace. But if we who read it are inspired by it, then a new creative venture may be the result.

He wrote his long letter to thank me because the translation of Rabindranath's poem was by me. He also hoped to be invited for small concerts in which he could relate his story. He wanted to know what other great sayings of Tagore could further guide him.

Unknown to us in India, Rabindranath works his magic in the life of people in faraway places and unlikely situations. I remember two instances when he rescued lives in Europe. During the First World War, an Indian soldier in the British Army was brought with both legs badly wounded. The German surgeon had to amputate them both to save the man's life. He wanted to gain the confidence and permission of the terror-struck soldier. There was no language between them. So the surgeon pronounced the one Indian name he knew,

'Rabindranath Tagore', three times. Listening to this name, the wounded man relaxed and nodded consent.

Again, during the Second World War a Polish doctor, Janusz Korczak, in charge of some 200 children, all living in the horrible conditions of the Warsaw Ghetto, staged Tagore's play 'The Post Office' with them–'to prepare them for the angel of death', for they were sure to be deported to a concentration camp soon.

We all receive scriptural or personal revelations, be they religious or spiritual, intuitive, emotional or intellectual, through the word. There must be many other such instances unknown to me where the power of the word had inspired and changed lives.

A Hermann Hesse Pilgrimage

Had we, as adolescents and young adults, not read Hermann Hesse's novels, our education and wordview would not have been complete. He was part of our life. Hesse occupies a bit the space of a cultural and spiritual Godfather in Germany like Rabindranath Tagore does in Bengal.

In India, the German writer Hermann Hesse (1877-1962) is best known as the author of his Indian novel, *Siddhartha.* It is not, as the name may suggest, modeled on the Buddha's life. Siddhartha is a Brahmin youth who decides to embrace the life of a wandering monk. After finding no happiness in it, he returns to the 'world' and becomes the lover of Kamala, a courtesan. Next, Siddhartha is the business partner of Kamaswami, an affluent businessman. Many years go by until Siddhartha realises that erotic love and wealth ultimately provide no lasting happiness and peace. He reverts to the ascetic life dwelling near a river as a boatsman.

Conrad Rooks' film *Siddhartha* (1972) with Shashi Kapoor in the role of Siddhartha, was shown in large cinema halls all over India and made Hesse's novel known to a wider Indian public. From this film emanated a genuinely Indian emotional atmosphere through its mystical landscapes. In long and quiet shots, it surveyed the area around Rishikesh for Siddhartha's youth; a magnificent Rajasthani fort for the 'wordly' episode with Kamala and Kamaswami; the Ganges, further downstream, with its plain and sparsely wooded terrain. The Indian public was able to find an entry into Hermann Hesse's mind through its own landscapes. Hence, the novel *Siddhartha* also attained a certain measure of fame in this country because many wanted to read the book after being moved by the film.

In the 1960s and 1970s, Indian adolescents, I hear, picked up *Siddhartha* from hippie young men and women who surged on to Indian shores from Europe and America. Many of them kept *Siddhartha* in their pockets like a life-saving medicine. But on the whole, it never was the cult book in India that it became in the West. Why should it? Does the Indian subcontinent not have its own share of inspirational literature?

Hermann Hesse's maternal grandfather, Hermann Gundert, was a Protestant Christian missionary in Kerala and is to this day respected for his research on the Malayalam language. Hesse's father and mother were missionaries in Kerala; his mother was born in Kerala. By the time Hermann Hesse war born, his grandfather and parents had already returned to Germany. During his youth, the young Hesse's imagination was fed on tales of life in India. Hesse was no adventurous traveler. He preferred a life of quiet contemplation. He only ventured out of Europe once, and that was in 1911 when he embarked on a long and arduous voyage to Asia. It took him to Ceylon (Sri Lanka), Kuala Lumpur, Singapore, Sumatra and back. On his return voyage he had planned to visit the mainland of India; but as he was sick, weary and disappointed, Hesse preferred to return straight to Europe. The voyage took slightly longer than three months.

No other German writer of repute has ever exposed himself so thoroughly to Indian thought as Hermann Hesse. He read Indian scriptures as soon as they appeared in German translation: the Upanishads, translated by Paul Deussen; the Bhagavad-Gita; several collections of the sermons of the Buddha, translated by Karl Eugen Neumann and Hermann Oldenberg which made a deep impression on the writer. He reviewed books with Indian content regularly (including three books by Rabindranath Tagore) and included several Indian classics in his 'Library of World Literature' which was a list of recommended writing. His yearning to fuse within himself the best of 'the East' with the best of Europe was so strong that he once recorded in a letter: 'Since many years I am convinced that the European mind is in the decline and is in need of a return to its Asian sources.' (1919).

Thus he became an eager and patient advocate of the classical Indian mind, without, of course, losing his appreciation for European culture. His ideas concerning the harmony of religions, with Christianity claiming no superior role, were far advanced for his time.

In Germany, Hesse's readership has become immense. In 2001, for example, 491,680 books by Hesse have been sold in German-speaking countries. In the rest of Europe and in North-America Hesse is the German author with the largest sale figure. Hermann Hesse would be little impressed by such statistics. He never strove to become a bestselling writer and he did nothing to further his popularity. Rarely did he venture out of his house to address the public; he had an hermitical bend of mind. He also forbade that films be made of his novels.

But he aspired to be a moral conscience-keeper of his people, or of anyone ready to listen to him and follow his rigorous standards of personal honesty and integrity. His message was age-old, as he repeated again and again: Be yourself, fulfill yourself in consonance with the universal will and with your love for humankind. He propagated the duty and right of every person to exercise his God-given freedom to find his own personal path in life, the *svadharma*, as we would say in India. With this moral authority Hesse uncompromisingly rejected the First World War despite the loud and enthusiastic war propaganda, and again the Second World War and the barbaric Hitler regime. He rejected the values of a contented bourgeois life, as much as the pleasures of money-making and power.

The enormous readership Hesse enjoys since the 1970s has a reverse side. Many academics do not consider Hesse a major writer. They dismiss him as too light, too sentimental, and too conventional. True, Hesse was a romantic and his style was never innovative. But the content of his novels, stories, poems, essays and of his over 35,000 letters reveal new and unexpected vistas for the consciousness of modern man. New editions of his most popular texts have been constantly published to satisfy the hunger for reading for especially young people who are about to mould their life, and of retired people who again have the leisure to contemplate the true values of their existence.

CALW

During my annual summer sojourn to Europe, it so happened that I visited several places where Hermann Hesse once lived. It felt like a pilgrimage. Hesse was born in the small town of Calw, close to the city of Stuttgart. Nestled in a narrow valley, Calw lines both sides of the small river Nagold and extends beyond the valley into the slopes. Even today, it is a picturesque town with many neatly maintained old houses. The writer's house of birth is on the small marketplace right in the centre of the town. Hermann Hesse has a large number of autobiographical writings to his credit, which sometimes are couched in fictional forms. The small-town mentality and narrow Christian piety Hesse experienced in his youth at Calw weighed him down, and he yearned at an early age to escape and breathe fresh air. The honourable citizens of Calw were none too pleased with these revelations and shunned Hesse. Even after his death, it took several decades until Calw's officialdom was able to accept their most famous son. At some stage, a bi-annual Hesse Symposium was initiated, a very well-equipped museum was opened near the birth-house, and a literary prize was instituted in Calw. Finally, it dawned on the municipality that Hesse does not only bestow honour on their town just by having been born in it, but that he has a market value as well. So on his 125th birth anniversary in 2002 and the 50th recurrence of his day of death in 2012, the town launched multiple events which attracted thousands of cultural tourists.

MAULBRONN

Maulbronn is the name of a medieval Cistercian monastery north of Stuttgart which was later converted into a Protestant school. This is where Hermann Hesse studied as a pupil from September 1891 for seven months. The narrow, sombre school atmosphere with its harsh, even cruel system of education and competitive, sometimes vindictive relationships was too much to bear for the sensitive adolescent. He fled and plunged into such deep depression that he attempted suicide and had to be treated in a home for mental patients. At this tender age, Hermann had already firmly resolved to 'become a writer and nothing else'. It was probably this desperate determination which helped him to overcome his crisis. Later he would write his famous novel *Under the Wheel* (1906) about his sufferings in Maulbronn. We in India are reminded of Rabindranath Tagore's experiences as a student in Kolkata. Both Hesse and Tagore left school without completing it. In his later life, Hesse however paid homage to Maulbronn when he elaborately described the monastery in another novel, *Narziss and Goldmund* (1930).

This marvelous, sprawling monastic compound of Maulbronn is a school even today. The medieval structure is intact making it one of the most amazing building complexes in Germany. Again, it took time for the authorities in Maulbronn to reconcile themselves to the 'bad name' Hesse had given its institution. But meanwhile, they, too, have come round and included Hermann Hesse in their many programmes and festivals which exploit the magnificent ambience.

MONTAGNOLA

Although Hermann Hesse was born in Germany and we are fond of calling him a 'German writer', yet he spent the longest part of his life in Switzerland and became a Swiss citizen. In 1912, he first settled in the Swiss capital, Berne, and from 1919 until his death in 1962, the writer stayed in Montagnola, situated in the Italian-speaking part of Switzerland called Ticino, close to the Italian border. Hesse was, again like Rabindranath, romantically in love with nature. So he chose a most attractive spot to spend the rest of his life. The two houses he occupied one after another, the Casa Camuzzi (until 1931) and the Casa Rossa, are on the top of a gently sloping mountain overlooking the town of Lugano and a large and lovely lake, besides numerous villages crouched in the wooded hills. Again and again Hesse expressed his gratitude to the Ticino mountainscape which never ceased to charm and inspire him.

Both, Rabindranath and Hesse, retired to their respective abodes of peace, to Shantiniketan and Montagnola, when they were about forty years of age, and spent another forty years amidst this self-chosen beauty. And both started to paint without formal training. Hesse lovingly produced one water-colour painting after another with Ticino landscapes, while Rabindranath chose to look within and draw out both his fairies and his demons and give them shape and colour.

When I visited my maternal ancestral home in Northern Italy, I decided with my two German companions, to visit Montagnola. They took me in their car for the two-hour drive along the magnificent Lago Maggiore into Switzerland. Approaching Lugano, I realised that this was no longer the landscape Hesse had loved and painted on paper. Lugano is now an industrial town; a broad and busy trunk road cuts through the length of the valley. When we stood near the Casa Camuzzi, the air reverberated with the muzzled noises of a hundred motors. Already during his lifetime, Hesse had bemoaned these deep transformations. What would he say today?

Both Hesse houses are in the possession of and occupied by families. Therefore they are not open to the public. Efforts had failed to buy the part of the Casa Camuzzi in which Hesse had lived. It was not possible to raise sufficient money. But a small museum was opened in the narrow building adjacent to it. Here I felt the spirit of this creative genius so intensely that it almost took my breath away. However, when looking for the Casa Rossa, we had difficulties in identifying it, half hidden as it is from the narrow approach road by trees and bushes. No plate at the gate, no indications whatsoever! Do the residents so much fear for their privacy?

On our way back down the hill, we stopped at the church of St. Abbondio and were impressed by the pointed cypresses surrounding the delicate building like watchmen. Next to the church we found the cemetary of St. Abbondio. It is Hermann Hesse's final resting place. The grave is indicated by an austere stone slab with Hesse's name chiselled on it. It lacks the pomposity of many other graves on this cemetery. Hermann Hesse had bought this tiny plot during his lifetime (as is the custom in Europe) and probably had a hand in the planning of its simple design. Only the bunches of flowers, some wilted, some still fresh, which admiring readers have placed on the grey stone, were certainly not planned by Hesse. The dialogue between the writer and his readers continues.

Vienna's Marriage with Tradition

Austria is a tiny country in central Europe. Geographically, it is smaller than West Bengal. Austria being landlocked and located in the centre of Europe, had to face a typical fate. From all directions it absorbed different cultures and has, to this day, to fight for its own unalienable identity.

When I tell my Austrian friends that in India we often confuse 'Austria' with 'Australia', they put on a wounded smile. For example, the influences of the great French cultural invasion over two hundred years ago still leave a visible and audible mark. The majority of public parks in Vienna bear the stamp of the geometrical, manicured garden art so beloved by erstwhile French royalty. The Austrian language continues to promote a large number of terms and expressions derived from the French. Similarly, influences from East Europe, from Italy and from Germany (with which Austria shares the language) abound.

Austria itself once was the centre of an empire, the Austrian-Hungarian Hapsburg monarchy which proudly called itself a *Vielvölkerstaat*, a 'country inhabited by many peoples'. Its territory extended towards the east and south of present-day Austria to what today are the Czech Republic, Slovakia, Croatia, Bosnia, to parts of Poland, Italy and Serbia. The days of the monarchy ended after the First World War, in 1918, when the last Kaiser abdicated the throne. Since then Austria is a truncated country. In 1938, Austria was annexed by Hitler in the infamous *Anschluss* which made Austria a part of Germany until 1945.

Save a few months, I have spent my entire university studies in Austria's capital, Vienna. I had begun my studies in a small German city near my home, but I felt unhappy there. At that time German students still followed the habit of spending one semester of their studies in a large European capital to absorb its range of high culture and broaden their experience.

So I decided to escape to Austria enjoying my 'cultural semester' much earlier than one was supposed to. I never left Vienna until completing my PhD! I went to a theatreplay, or an opera, or a concert, or a poetry reading, or a dance performance every single evening. I experienced large portions of the European theatre and concert repertoire in world-class performances.

How was this possible on a slim student budget? It was possible with the help of an institution in Vienna theatre and concert halls called *Stehplatz*, 'standing space'. These halls keep an area reserved for people standing through the performance. They lean on a railing, but get no seat, to save space. Obviously, we did not mind standing through even the six-hour performance of a Wagner opera because the tickets, obtained from a university office, just cost the price of two cups of coffee.

How can a country so small offer 'world-class' culture? Because of its imperial traditions. When you walk through Vienna you do not see the modest capital of a country of merely 8.3 million people. You see grand architecture fit to demonstrate the might and self-esteem of a large monarchy. You have those expansive French-style parks, like Belvedere and Schönbrunn, those monumental cathedrals like Stefansdom and Karlskirche, a sprawling imperial castle, the Hofburg. You have two big, old-style opera houses, and the Burgtheater which is the premier German-speaking theatre, as well as many other signs of old grandeur.

Austria relives its international importance by cultivating its heritage with a discerning love for tradition. The empire may have gone, but the opera remains imperial. A Vienna proverb says: 'A crisis in the management of the opera house is worse than a government crisis.' This interface between tradition and modernity has its distinct charm. For example, as a mark that monarchism is passé all titles of nobility have been banned. No titles must be mentioned publicly. You are just 'Mr' and 'Mrs'. Yet, if we listen closely to conversations in Vienna, we hear people being addressed as 'Baroness' or 'Count'. Under the surface, aristocratic symbols and mannerisms are in vogue. Men gallantly kiss the hand of ladies with a deep bow reminiscent of aristocratic demeanour. Memories of the 'K.u.K. (*Kaiserliche und Königliche*) Monarchy' abound when you stroll around in Vienna. For example, the inheritors of the erstwhile imperial suppliers of pastries continue to call themselves *K.u.K. Zuckerbäcker*.

Possibly, the vanished empire has left a sense of loss, a loneliness and melancholy in the Austrian character. To this day, its literature is replete with black humour, with caustic, self-depreciating wit, and a fatalistic passion for imagining gloomy narratives around loss, transience and death.

Do I imagine it, or is it true that there are some distinctive similarities between the huge India and the small Austria? India, too, is truncated and continues to suffer from the trauma of partition. India was and is a *Vielvölkerstaat* taking pride in a multi-lingual and multi-ethnic national identity. As in Austria, large sections of India's society continue to dwell mentally in the feudal era of *rajas* and *ranis*. The most apparent similarity is, however, the love for music. An educated Kolkata boy or girl is likely to grow up singing and listening to Rabindra Sangeet. Likewise, Vienna bursts at the seams with Mozart and operettas, with waltzes and the more folksy *Schrammelmusik*. Music binds Austrian people together.

Outside the inner city, the streets of Vienna used to appear glum and dreary. Unimaginative social housing projects had spread everywhere. Now even these fringes of the city bear a much brighter look. Historical buildings have been carefully renovated. For example, the suburban railway stations have mostly been maintained in their characteristic *Jugendstil*, a style which developed in the early 20th century. The city has gained much from its renewed international flair. The United Nations have made Vienna one of its European centres. Vienna continues to remain the gate to East Europe, especially after the Iron Curtain has been dismantled and borders have become porous.

Looking at the crumbling palaces of old Kolkata we are forced to acknowledge that Austria is far advanced in its will to preserve tradition. This is not merely a matter of funds. With a strong sense of history people can generate a will to overcome obstacles and maintain the manifestations of certain venerable traditions.

When I completed my studies in Vienna, I immediately prepared to depart for India to teach German at the Ramakrishna Mission Institute of Culture in Kolkata. That was in 1973. After that, whenever I returned to Germany, I made it a point to visit Vienna. I do my work during the day, and from the late afternoons I merge with the cultural life of the city, enjoying thoroughly the homecoming to my student days. I roam through some nooks and corners which I never miss to look up. There is the *Judenplatz* (Jewish Square) which allows no traffic, hence it is quiet and serene; there is the coffee house at the *Schwarzenbergplatz* where you sip coffee which is served with a glass of plain water to balance the bitterness of coffee. These coffee houses play no music and have no television sets. Instead they keep a bunch of daily newspapers which you can take to your table and read. Even if you take two hours over a cup of coffee while reading ten newspapers, the waiter will never be disgruntled. There have been writers in Vienna who did the bulk of their writing in a coffee house which they frequented daily. They did not even hesitate to direct their letters and visitors to their coffee house. It is comforting to return to a city and realise that certain things do not change.

HOLDING FAST TO THE PAST

When I visited Vienna in July 2011, the oldest son of the last emperor of the Habsburg monarchy, Otto von Habsburg, passed away near Munich. He was 98. Had the monarchy not been abandoned in the aftermath of the First World War and Austria not turned into a republic, Otto von Habsburg would have ascended the throne as the Kaiser of Austria and the King of Hungary. Instead he, as a boy of six, had to flee with his family to a Portuguese island in the Atlantic Ocean and begin a restless life wandering from one European country to another and to the US where his children now live.

Even when western Europe entered an uninterrupted era of peace after the Second World War, Otto was unable to return home, to the city of Vienna. Fearful that he may fuel a movement propagating a return to monarchic rule, Austria wanted him to renounce his claims in writing which Otto did only as late as 1961. Even then, squabbles and misgivings prevented the former Crown Prince from settling down in Austria. Instead, he became a German citizen and lived near Munich.

For twenty years, he served as a Member of the European Parliament. He fought for European unity and became one of the persons responsible for the fall of the Iron Curtain. He worked for human rights especially in East Europe, the erstwhile territory of the monarchy. During the Nazi regime, he refused to meet Adolf Hitler, although invited, and during Communist rule, he fought Communist totalitarianism. Highly educated, multi-lingual, a statesman-like political figure, revered and reviled alike, he for over half a century was a persistent presence in public life.

It was sheer good luck that I happened to visit Vienna when Otto von Habsburg received his ceremonial burial in the crypt of the Kapuzinerkirche, the church of the Capuchin monks, which for many centuries has been the last resting place of numerous emperors and kings. It was highly educative how Austrian society threw to the winds all reservations about the monarchy and celebrated its past with sombre abandon. On the days preceding the burial, the coffin was displayed in the Kapuzinerkirche. A long line of people wound their way inside to pay their respects to the deceased. They were not merely diehard monarchists who see everything good that ever happened in the past. The majority were young people with children and middle-aged couples.

The coffin was guarded by men in historical uniforms and helmets which somehow had survived since the First World War. The guards looked a bit like playing roles in a historical costume film. But more important to me was to notice that the crowds were patient and carried themselves with dignity. No scuffles, no loud voices, no wails and no sobbing; nobody creating a 'scene'. The atmosphere was prayerful and serene.

On Saturday, 16 July, a festive church service was conducted in the St. Stephen's Cathedral of Vienna, attended by one thousand invited guests from all over Europe. Thereafter the coffin was carried through the streets of the central part of Vienna to the Kapuzinerkirche. Now that Otto von Habsburg was dead, unable to claim imperial power or prestige, all the symbols and paraphernalia of imperial glory could be exhibited without reservation. Long rows of people in the uniforms of traditional organisations and orders, some with capes, banners or staffs and various other insignia marched behind the coffin. A military band was playing.

Once the coffin arrived at the gate of the Kapuzinerkirche, an age-old ritual dialogue was enacted one last time. The herald knocked at the gate with his staff. The voice of a monk was heard: 'Who is there?' And the herald would in a long litany reel off all the titles Otto had or would have had. 'I know him not!' came the answer. Once again the herald tried, listing all the orders and associations of which Otto had been a member. The same answer followed. Finally, the herald announced: 'This is Otto, a sinful and mortal human being.' After this the gate opened and the coffin was ushered inside.

The Catholic Church, a spiritual as well as a political power during the monarchy, was able to reveal its spiritual side as well as its worldly glitz. Even though it tells us that we are but poor, mortal men and women, a dozen bishops and prelates, in splendid violet attire, followed the coffin.

The bells of the many churches lining the streets began to toll as the procession approached. With its churches and monasteries half-empty and people who are still believers, turning to less ceremonious expressions of faith, I enjoyed witnessing that the Church's colourful and festive ceremonies continue to hold a spell on the population.

Some newspapers wallowed in scorn and ridicule about this show of imperial and ecclesiastical grandeur. But the people in the procession who participated were serious and dedicated. It did not have the air of a costume party or a carnival, and I felt no fanaticism. This pomp reminded me again of the fact that Austria, after all, was a truncated country. Its spectacular imperial buildings the Hofburg, the Opera House, the Burgtheater, the museums, the Ring Street with its parks and institutions of the state and of culture encircling the inner city, are too extravagant for a country with a population of merely 8.3 million people. That is about as many as greater Kolkata.

True, such a show of imperial grandeur seems pointless and is potentially dangerous as the persons behind it crave to hold back the irreversible march towards modern life. But it is equally true that they reveal a deep human yearning for continuity, for constancy, for something to hold on to in the confusion of modern life. Raising it to a higher level, we are here confronted by the deeply felt human need for certainty within the fleeting flow of time. It is a possibly unconscious and impotent attempt to grasp eternity within our time-bound life. We have no right to scorn or ridicule it.

Scotland's Mystery of Open Spaces

For decades I believed that the quest for beautiful landscapes and for other liberating experiences should be pursued in the south. This is a typical German attitude. For over two hundred years, German people have idolised Italy and Greece not only as the foundations of ancient European culture. The Mediterranean region also became identified with sun and warmth, with lovely scenery, monumental architecture and with carefree men and women. Our classical writer, Johann Wolfgang Goethe, had escaped from the foggy North to Rome in order to find solace, and generation after generation of writers, artists, musicians and bon vivants followed. To this day, the German colony of cultural people in Italy is plentiful.

THE REVELATION OF THE NORTH

I reversed my attitude when I first visited Edinburgh in the year 2000. I had read an advertisement in a British newspaper about a fellowship which Hawthornden Castle in Scotland awarded to published writers. I applied and stayed for one month in this lovely medieval castle just a few miles outside Edinburgh. I did my writing and explored the countryside. I realised that the North of Europe has its distinct charm as well. The small hamlets nestling in an undulating landscape, the 'glens' (as the steep gorges are called) and the castles perched on hillocks create a paradise for artists and poets. Coming from India, however, another feature of the Scottish landscape fascinated me the most. That was the vast expanse of virtual emptiness that I encountered north to Edinburgh, in the so-called Highlands.

After my first visit to Scotland, I would return almost every year for a week's vacation. My friend Jeanne Openshaw, who until recently taught Anthropology at the University of Edinburgh, and I explored the western coast with a variety of islands grouped in front of it, called the Hebrides. Once we took the train to the farthest north, to a place called Thurso and then ferried across to the Orkney Isles. In another year, we discovered the north-western coast between Ullapool and Lochinver. What fascinated me was that we could travel for hours without passing through a town. On both sides of the train track or the bus route, we saw a seemingly endless expanse of hills and valleys, often denuded since centuries. A glorious monotony accentuated by the 'lochs' (as the lakes are called), a landscape dotted only by sheep and occasional small settlements.

This stark landscape is covered by hard grass which the sheep eat, often by moors and heath. If you add the often strong winds to this picture, the cold yet brilliant sun or the low-sailing heavy clouds, then you have an environment of rugged austerity. Coming from the overpopulated plains of India with its luxuriously rich vegetation, traveling in the Scottish Highlands feels like a cleansing of the soul. Where else in Europe do we still get this feeling of space, this sense of freedom? This boundless emptiness is not dead like a desert would be, but it vibrates with an inner life, with a serene, unflappable charm. Maybe it is the quality of the eternal which attracts me. Apart from the Highlands, I have experienced it only in certain parts of the Himalayas. But there it is less accessible. I seem to need it once a year, as a kind of antidote, before I relocate to Golden Bengal.

When we took a train to the north of Scotland, it was a small-gauge single-track route, the only one existing to the extreme north. It felt like being a pioneer exploring still untraced areas. And when we reached the ocean, it was like arriving at the end of the world. Crossing over to the mainland of the Orkney Islands, we cycled to the Ring of Brodgar which is an ancient ring of standing stones. Within a wide, level landscape, limited only by the equally wide and level sea, stand those huge stones. They are the only vertical lines in the horizontal world of Orkney. They have such power, such energy! They show what the spirit of man can do to make its presence felt surrounded by a harsh nature inimical to the comforts of human habitation.

The same magic revealed itself when we visited Achiltibue in the north-west. Situated on the craggy coast of the mainland

and overlooking a varied group of islands called the Summer Isles, this small village commands a breathtaking vista. Here are the ocean, the islands, and the rolling hills with a few steep mountains receding into the blue horizon of the mainland. We are reminded of human habitation by just a few of those sturdy white houses, built to withstand the gales and the winter cold and accentuated by their two chimneys, one on each side of the roof.

Jeanne and I talked to as many local people as possible. Mrs Muir, a shopkeeper who also leases out a cottage to summer guests, shares our view about the glory of the land and waterscape. She, however, continues with a 'but'. The winters are harsh. They are dark and dreary. It rains and rains. The few hours of daylight are dull. Many people tend to resign themselves to the bottle and to depression.

When we returned to the capital, the Edinburgh Festival was about to start. I realised that it is the major cultural event of the year, spanning the entire month of August. It has mainly two parts, the official, highbrow programme of theatre plays, concerts, art shows, and the so-called 'Fringe'. This is a conglomeration of events mostly by lesser-known artists who perform partly in open spaces or in the streets or on temporary makeshift stages. The entire city seems to be sucked into a festival fever. There is no way to dodge the crowds or ignore the festival.

Before leaving for the airport to return to Germany, I sat for a while in the park alongside Princes Street. From there I had a view of Edinburgh Castle and its surrounding old and narrow houses. Edinburgh seems to breathe an air of freedom reminiscent of the Highlands. It has no maze of cramped and jammed streets and lanes like other major cities. Edinburgh is spread out between the ocean, called here the Firth of Forth, and a hillock, named Arthur's Seat.

A few wide avenues crossing the city from west to east, especially the Royal Mile, give a rather clear structure to the city centre. More importantanly, it lends to the city some impressive perspectives. Looking down on the ocean from the Royal Mile gives you a feeling of space which perhaps no other European capital can offer. The uninhabited Holyrood Park with the Arthur's Seat as its summit creates the impression as if you were not in a city at all.

On the other hand, Edinburgh abounds in houses with dark exteriors. Have the walls darkened from age or is their stone of that colour? These gloomily dark facades combined with the architecturally typical small turrets, steeples, alcoves, niches and tiny windows give you the eerie impression of things hidden, of mysteries waiting to unfold.

Passing by the small café where J.K. Rowling wrote her first Potter novel, I began to understand the connection between the Potter Magic and the city where these novels were created. But what is the connection between these houses with their complicated micro-structure and the wide openness of the Highlands? There is mystery in both of them. There is charm in both. But how do these opposites connect? This is yet another mystery.

A VISIT TO THE ISLAND OF IONA

What is 'magical'? Obviously, I do not speak here of black magic, that is sorcery, nor of white magic of the kind P.C. Sorcar produces. Rather, I speak of the enigmatic attraction which certain spaces and moments of time have for us personally and may not exist for others. Certain key events become magical—our marriage, or the birth of a child, a ritual or ceremony of special significance. In our memory many events, even though ordinary when we live through them, obtain a magical glow. Or a trip which perhaps began as something commonplace and suddenly evolved into an enchanting and captivating experience.

One such trip was to the Scottish isle of Iona. Jeanne and I travelled from Edinburgh by train up to Oban, crossed over to the Isle of Mull by a car-ferry, continued to Fionnphort by bus and then crossed the Sound of Iona on board a much smaller car-ferry to the island of Iona. It measures just three miles in length and one mile across.

Some say that such magic emanates from history, from peoples who once lived at that place, from kings and their vassals, from the rituals they once performed and so on. This may be so. Undisputable, however, is that age helps to create the atmosphere which a place radiates. History tells us that the first peoples to move into Scotland were the Celts. It is safe to say that they inhabited Iona by the year 3000 BC. First they were nomads, later they settled to engage in agriculture. Today, little is left to give witness to those times—some stones overgrown by grass. In our modern era, a Christian missionary,

Columba, voyaged from nearby Ireland to Iona and settled there. He died in 563 after spending 34 years on the isle where he built up a vigorous monastic centre. He seems to have been one of those energetic and charismatic figures who leave their mark on an entire age with their zeal to mould the religious, social and cultural life of the people around them.

Later, an abbey was built by Benedictine monks and monastic life continued until the Reformation. After that the Abbey Church and its adjacent buildings as well as a nunnery gradually slid towards decrepitude. About a hundred years ago, however, the Abbey Church began to be rebuilt by a trust and given to all Christian dominations for worship. Care was taken that the Church was being restored largely as it stood in the Middle Ages while it was part of a Benedictine monastery. The Abbey Church is today the focus of Iona's social life. A community has gathered around it whose members and guests visit the island regularly for spiritual retreats. Dozens of these pilgrims can find shelter in a few guest houses.

When we visited the isle in October, the summer season had just come to an end. We saw not more than two dozen pilgrims. The benign weather had made room for an unpredictable stormy climate with intermittent rain lashing the landscape. In such conditions, the small ferry can no longer control the high waves and manage the landing at the *ghats*. It has to remain tied down in a bay near Fionnphort. Then Iona is cut off. When we arrived, the ferry had not operated the previous day and the weather forecast for the next few days was not promising. Yet, we availed of the last crossing of the day while the waves were relatively smooth.

The island, covered by verdant green grass and various rock formations, is crowned by a hillock, the Dun I. There are just a few trees around the village, called Baile Mor. It consists of a few houses along two roads. Only the cars of its one hundred and twenty inhabitants are allowed on the island. So there is no traffic to speak of. Iona does have electricity and sufficient potable water, both supplied from across the Sound.

The stark barrenness of the island captivated me as soon as we landed. People who love Iona, had told me of its 'beauty'. But what is 'beautiful' about an island so barren, so lonely, so much victim of the elements? During the two days we stayed on Iona I discovered a new meaning of beauty. The utter simplicity of the island–its size, its uniform landscape, its emptiness: few people, few animals, few houses, little of all things–made it easy to existentially inhabit the island. By 'inhabit' I here mean that I spread my feelings and thoughts and my entire being across the island and 'live it'. These are upanishadic reflections which emerged spontaneously in Iona.

When I described the isle as being a 'victim of the elements', I viewed the situation in negative terms. But staying on I realised that it need not be a negative situation at all to live among the elements, fierce though they might be. On that day, strong winds which almost swept us off our feet reigned over the isle. Its bareness was an open invitation to the winds to roam freely. Every now and then, they suddenly brought along icy rain which attacked us sideways and hit our face like pin pricks. Jeanne and I were on our way to the northern tip, beyond the narrow metal road, beyond a modest youth hostel tucked behind a hill. But we had to give up and return to the Argyll Hotel for fear of getting all drenched. We were not robust enough for the fury of the elements.

Due to its simplicity, everything I did on Iona, congealed in my imagination into a symbol. The walk to the north took on the contours of life's journey with its rapidly changing 'weather'–its successes and failures. And this is where I see the beauty of Iona. It contains within its narrow confines the possibility to experience much that is essential in our life by transcending the mere materiality of the isle and understanding it as a symbol. This process came natural and made the visit to Iona precious.

The Abbey Church is part of this elementary feeling. Although erected so recently, it is assembled of ancient stones from the area, possibly many even taken from the ruins of the medieval structure. Its form is modest, but powerful, it renounces all ornamental trappings, all superfluous elegance. It is straight and solid like a rock rising from the ground. The raw and rough texture of the stones stacked in layer upon layer merge beautifully with the surrounding landscape. I was not astonished to hear that the dead from Mull and other places outside the island were transferred to Iona to be buried next to the Abbey Church. In this ancient ground, they found their adequate resting place.

What is 'magical'? It is when the inner being sees itself all of a sudden mirrored and surprisingly expressed in the outside world. The German word *Seelenlandschaft* is appropriate here: the 'landscape of the soul'. You go somewhere, experience a landscape or make the acquaintance of a person, and what do you discover? Yourself; your Self. That is magical.

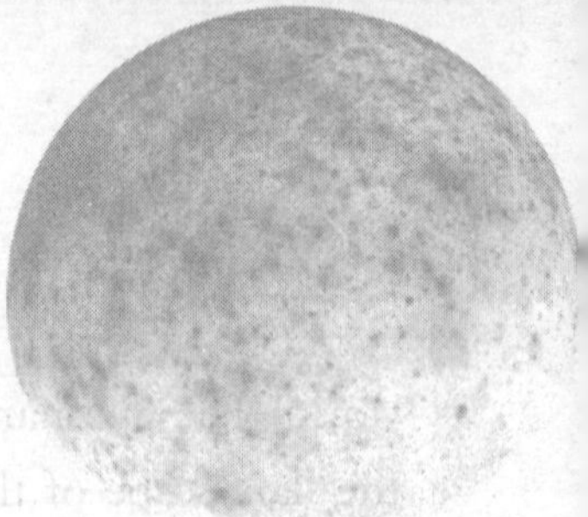

Rome's Lovely Street Cafés

Where does the fascination of this city come from? Is it Rome's antiquity going back several thousand years? Or its imperial, often cruel, often superbly creative, past–its imperious statesmen, its remnants of the Renaissance with its visions of universality and genius? Is it the attraction of a modern city, one of Europe's commercial and fashion hubs? Is it its famously good food and ice cream? Well, it is all of these, and more! It is the comfortable blending of antiquity and modernity, of ancient pride with rustic, joyous simplicity, of the bonhomie generated by elegant living with the poverty of the immigrant population. But foremost it is this astounding cooperation between the monuments of the past and a busy, irreverent modern life!

I stayed in the via del Corso, one of the large thoroughfares, cutting through the old city centre from north to south. Close to the Piazza del Popolo, squeezed between the avenue's eastern row of houses, is the Casa di Goethe, the Goethe House where I occupied a room. This is where Johann Wolfgang Goethe, Germany's foremost classical writer, lived, escaping from the severity of his duties at the Weimar court and from the foggy climate of the north. The German government acquired the flat and turned it into a cultural centre where exhibitions, lectures and discussions are being organised in Italian or German.

The via del Corso is thronged by tourists during most of the day as it leads to several tourist sites. I try to avoid places which tourists frequent. For how can we imbibe the spirit of any ancient location when we have several hundred competitors? It is as absurd as watching the sunrise on Darjeeling's Tiger Hill among a throng of people eagerly *oh*-ing and *ah*-ing at the first glimmer of light. Any historical site emanates its particular aura. We need a contemplative attitude and a certain solitude and isolation to absorb and to profit from it.

I discovered a way out. That was to cruise Rome's popular avenues early morning, at six or seven, when tourists were still asleep. The early mornings find Rome belonging to the native people occupied with their routine jobs, like walking their dog, going on their round of jogging, buying a daily newspaper, attending early mass in one of the numerous churches, and sipping a first cup of coffee to become fully awake.

Between the via del Corso and the spacious hilly park area surrounding the Villa Borghese, I discovered a criss-cross of narrow lanes which are frequented by few outsiders throughout the day. Here, it seemed, the arty, bohemian local population had settled in. Studios, galleries, art shops dotted the roadside.

On the via Belsiana, I discovered a coffee shop which opens early and caters to workmen. A few tiny tables covered by bright red soiled cloths had been placed on the road. I sat down and ordered a cappuccino with a croissant and a toasted cheese sandwich for breakfast. Leisurely, I watched life pass by. The young men with their lively faces and expressive gestures sauntered in to gulp a quick espresso, they greeted their chums and ran off to their places of work. Outside, vehicles brought new supplies for shops, and the sweepers were busy clearing the garbage and washing the cobble-stoned road.

It was the same routine every morning. On the second day a sweeper, recognising me, nodded into my direction, and on my forth and last day, he saluted me with a raised hand. Equally, on the third morning the elderly, grumpy owner of the coffee shop no longer asked what I wanted, he just brought it to me. This is what I love–bonding with the population in tiny but, to me, significant ways, establishing a belonging of sorts. This is how the pulse of a city can be felt–not by goggling at some new monuments every day, but by watching the same scene at the same place day after day. These street cafés tucked away in some secret lane are truly idyllic. I sit there and become part of life, and yet I observe life as if from outside. I survey the hectic or joyous pace around me, and yet I do not get sucked in. My coffee shop was cheap, too. I paid just six euro for my breakfast. Contrast this to the restaurants on the Plaza del Popolo, for instance, where one cup of cappuccino alone costs you 5.50 euro.

Sitting outside to eat and drink is an established Mediterranean habit. People in Italy and Greece yearn to live outside as much as possible. As soon as winter has departed, tables are placed outside for meals and coffee. The sun, the unclouded blue skies are precious and so deeply anticipated in Europe. This southern habit has travelled northward in the past several decades. As a boy I never sat outside to eat or have coffee and cake. Nowadays, a café without a garden to sit in or an enclosed patch along the street is doomed to do unsatisfactory business.

India with her abundance of sunshine obviously cannot appreciate this European yearning. To us in India, a good life means to be closeted inside air-conditioned coolness. Mosquitoes, the dust of the road, the crowds passing by, and concern for ritual purity rather discourage city people from open-air eating and living. By contrast, in Rome restaurant tables are squeezed precariously in between house walls and people flood by in between cars, honking motorbikes spewing toxic fumes and people standing around, noisily chattering and gesticulating. But nobody seems to mind.

In the evenings, Rome explodes with the grateful bustle of a day's work completed. Then, visitors and inhabitants do mix with ease. The Romans offer and sell, or relax and squabble, enjoy a meal, and play with their children, supremely undisturbed by camera-wielding tourists.

Never visit a city where you have no friends! I have followed this motto throughout my decades of travelling. In India, it is not only a privilege but a necessity to have contacts in a new city. No Indian family would normally venture out to a place totally devoid of a welcome. At the airport of Rome, Alice met me. The young Italian anthropologist had spent several months at our Santal village, Ghosaldanga, near Shantiniketan working on her dissertation. Her eyes still become moist when she enquires about the children, her faraway friends. She and her partner, Daniele, took me one evening to the outskirts of Rome to have a rustic meal among the locals. Here the menu card was printed only in Italian—no English for the tourists!

On Sunday, I went to the Abbey of San Anselmo perched serenely on top of one of the seven hills of Rome. The Latin mass was recited by the Benedictine monks who hailed from different continents. The Gregorian chant, simple, almost monotonous, but so exhilaratingly beautiful in its unhurried flow and sweep, filled the church like angles' voices. Abbot Notker Wolf met me after mass. He is a leading spiritual writer and the head of some 20,000 monks and nuns in the whole world. Yet, his demeanour was simple and jovial, devoid of suggestions of pride and prestige. What a joy to know people who have remained simple, who have the courage to be just themselves! Thinking of the workmen in the coffee shop and its owner, of Alice and Daniele, and Notker filled me with gratitude when I returned to Germany.

When the Berlin Wall Fell

Mahatma Gandhi would have been elated. The wall separating East Berlin and West Berlin was the symbol of the division between the dictatorial, not free eastern bloc and the democratic, free western world. It was a stark symbol which revealed the naked truth of the captivity suffered by the people in Communist countries. The wall fell, thanks to a peaceful mass movement, and demonstrated that freedom cannot be contained forever.

Mahatma Gandhi was always looking for strong symbols of evil power which he strove to break with the 'soul power' of *ahimsa*. He went on his carefully orchestrated Salt March to demonstrate to the world what a crowd adamant to keep peace could accomplish. Similarly, the crowds of people in East Berlin and Leipzig who demonstrated against an evil regime in 1989 were determined to remain peaceful. They shouted 'No violence!' and marched on. So far, the police had fought against street demonstrations. They beat up protesters and jailed them. On 9 October 1989, 70,000 people moved on the streets of Leipzig's inner city towards the Nikolai Church. What happened was most unexpected: the state police, for the first time, offered no resistance. This was the signal event which led, exactly a month later, to the fall of the Berlin Wall.

The state realised in October that the patience of the population had worn thin. It demanded the freedom, it demanded the prosperity enjoyed by the citizens in West Germany. The Polish uprising had preceded these events. Hungary had opened its borders to Austria and tens of thousands of East Germans fled to West Germany. Gorbachov, the Soviet leader, advocated political liberation through *glasnost* and *perestroika*. He visited East Berlin and pronounced those ominous words: 'Whoever comes too late, will be punished by life itself.' The regime had to take some steps. Its strongman Erich Honecker resigned. His successor promised reforms. But this decision came too late. A weakened political system was unable to renew itself and pacify the swelling masses on the streets.

However, even a month prior to the opening of the Berlin Wall, the dissolution of the East German regime and the unification of Germany were neither discussed nor demanded by the masses. All they had wanted were reforms and the freedom to travel. They were no empty dreamers reaching out for the impossible. So when the impossible did happen, it took everybody by surprise: the protesters, the Communist regime and the West German government. When on 9 November, 1989, the Berlin Wall opened and the East German population flocked into the West by the thousands, it appeared like a miracle.

Was the East German state actually prepared to give itself up? Unchecked freedom of movement evidently entailed the admission that the German Democratic Republic (GDR) has become ungovernable. One hole in the Wall was enough to secure that freedom, just like one flicker of light is enough to light up a dark room. The sequence of events leading to the opening of the Wall has never been totally clarified. However, one thing is certain: the opening was the result of a misunderstanding within the confused and panicky East Berlin administration.

Somebody voiced an opinion which was misinterpreted and then handed down as a command to the border police force which acted upon it without cross-checking. It is hard to believe, but to a certain extent the dissolution of the Eastern bloc was the consequence of a blunder committed by some middle-rung *apparatchik* in East Berlin.

I happened to be in West Germany at the time. I sat in front of the television all day following the live broadcast with bated breath. The exhilaration of the crowds, jumping on to the top of the Wall, dancing on the symbol of evil, cannot be imagined, it could only be witnessed.

Once the Wall had been broken open, nothing could stop the people from forcing other passages through the Wall. On television, we saw hundreds of people with pickaxes hacking away and reducing segments of the Wall to rubble. These were people from both the East and the West of Berlin. There was a high power synergy at work bringing men and women from East and West together. Unknown people fell into each other's arms, sang together and celebrated.

The alacrity of the West German government astonished me. The very next day, Chancellor Helmut Kohl and the entire political establishment from all parties congregated in front of the Wall near the Brandenburg Gate. Then and there, Kohl announced the unification of the two Germanys. With sure political instinct, he seized the auspiciousness of the moment to 'bind together what belongs together'. Countless West German youths simply jumped into their cars and drove to Berlin to participate in the big party.

From that day onwards, East Germans were free to enter the West at will. But they had no money, as their currency counted for nothing outside its territory. They were given 100 Deutsche Mark on every visit so they could buy at least a meal, a beer and some souvenirs. It is mind-boggling to even consider the difficulties which then arose in integrating two opposed social and political systems which had existed isolated from each other for the last forty years. But the rush towards unification became so forceful that in less than a year, on 3 October 1990, the two countries officially became one political entity.

It is my good luck that I had been able to visit the GDR in 1988, a year before its dissolution. As a West German, I was not permitted to simply travel to the eastern part of Germany. I either had to prove that I had relatives there, or that I was invited by an official agency. That year, a German publisher in Leipzig wanted to bring out my stories on India. They had been previously published in West Germany, but as West German books could not be bought in the GDR, they wanted, after due government permission, to bring out their own edition. I was invited to visit them and discuss the details. In the West, a two-hour discussion with a representative of the publishing house would have settled everything, and if the author is lucky, he or she would be invited for a meal afterwards. In the GDR work was slow-paced because unemployment was ruled out; everybody was supposed to do something to get a salary. Competition was unknown. The result was that the representative of the publisher leisurely showed me around the country for a full week. I walked down the desolate, dreary streets of East Berlin. Most of its facades still bore the holes created during the Second World War by bomb splinters and grenade shelling. Restaurants and cafés did not exist except a very few state-run establishments with monotonous food choices. When I ran out of tissue paper to blow my nose, no new supply was available in any of the shops. The Main Station of Leipzig is the biggest in Germany. It was pathetic to see it had no shops, no restaurants, no colour. Just drabness under a vast overarching steel structure! It is hard to describe the feelings of commiseration with the people who spoke the same language as I, and of relief when I returned by train from Berlin to Hamburg.

The initial enthusiasm over the unexpected unification gone, some of the baser instincts took charge, especially greed.

East Germans were exposed to the consumerist West and many fell for it headlong. They wanted to catch up with western society in the shortest possible time. Vice-versa, commercially-minded people of the West rushed into the East to establish branches of their businesses, to buy up land and houses–to enhance their wealth mostly at the expense of East German citizens who did not have the money power to operate on the same level. Such uncloaked display of greed marred my joy of no longer having to write 'West Germany' on my letter envelopes, but merely 'Germany'.

After a few years, many people in the East began to forget the suppression and suffering and only remembered the positive aspects of their former life: job security, an assured place in the local kindergarten for their children, free basic medical treatment and some such benefits. Now they had to be competitive for everything they got. Many succeeded in building a new life, others did not. Many lost their jobs because their factories or businesses could not compete with the superior production and skill of West Germans. Hundreds of thousands left the East to settle in the West. In my small home town, Boppard, a taxi business was taken over by several young people from Berlin. My family doctor is from the former GDR. They have been singularly successful in their profession and are integrated well.

The past two decades have seen, on the whole, a colossal improvement in the living standard of the East. When you take a car around the city you hardly recognise the transition from one part to another. I normally ask my taxi driver to point out the former position of the Wall. Sometimes it is drawn on the pavement and roads, often it is not. Occasionally though, you still see those decrepit, bullet-hole riddled facades typical of the GDR which remind us of the devastation wrought by the Second World War decades ago. Not all houses have been renovated yet. I also revisited Leipzig and arrived there by train. I could hardly recognise the huge space of the Main Station which had become vibrant with shopping malls, restaurants and lots of colour. A generation now comes of age which has not lived with the Wall. It has from birth enjoyed the fruits of freedom. But sections of the Wall have been preserved and rebuilt as memorials; the famous Checkpoint Charlie, a military transition point, has been turned into a museum.

Even if the living standard has dramatically improved, East and West have not yet united into one indivisible whole. Experts have recently said that it will take approximately fifty years to tide over all the differences and divisions. The Wall, a common adage says, has moved from the ground into the minds of people (*die Mauer im Kopf*). People are still identified as 'those from the East' (*Ossis*) and 'those from the West' (*Wessis*) with clichéd and sometimes derogatory emotional values attached to each term.

Meanwhile, the literature on the East-West dichotomy which has sprung up since 1989 can well fill a library. With heavy sincerity the German people are again engaged in what it has been engaged in since the disasters of the Second World War: *Vergangenheitsbewältigung*. That is, the process of coming to terms with one's own guilty past. First the reference was to the

Jewish extermination in the concentration camps and to the World War which Hitler's regime launched. Now it means the coming to terms with the evils of the Communist regime and the people's tacit collaboration with oppression and injustice.

For me, the one significant aspect of the 1989 events in Leipzig, Dresden, Berlin and elsewhere is that they had their foundation in the message of peace and non-violence. The prayers for peace which were held each Monday, the frequent peaceful demonstrations in the summer and autumn of 1989 did not follow one particular leader, like Mahatma Gandhi spearheaded *ahimsa* in India. Several courageous men and women of the Protestant Church gave direction and spiritual content to these demonstrations. The churches in the GDR never had it easy under the atheistic regime, and the majority of its inhabitants grew up indifferent to religion. But the peaceful dissolution of the GDR in 1989, religion played a decisive and positive role–like in India, led by Mahatma Gandhi; like in the US where Martin Luther King, a pastor, inspired the movement against racial discrimination; like in South Africa where Desmond Tutu, a pastor, was a force in the battle against apartheid.

About the Author

Martin Kämpchen was born in Germany in 1948 and has been living in India for the last 40 years. Widely travelled, even as student, his education spread over the continents, from the US to Vienna and Paris, and from Chennai to Santiniketan. He has a PhD each in Literature and Comparative Religion.

An acclaimed journalist, translator and editor he has written and published extensively, in both German and English, on Indian culture and is today considered an important cultural link between India and Germany.

Since 1980, Santiniketan has been his base from where he has translated the *Shri Ramakrishna Kathamrita* as well as Rabindranath Tagore's poems, from Bengali to German. His book *Simply Do It: Do It Simply* was published in 2013, by Niyogi Books.

'Martin Kämpchen pursues the events of daily life. He discovers that all things and actions that evolve around us are more than their mere appearance. Be it climbing steps in Rome, travelling by train, flying by plane and being silent, or speaking and even shedding tears, Kämpchen makes us readers sensitive to the seemingly minor, but essential significance of each activity and opens the way to our fulfillment as human beings–he unfolds a true Art of Life.'

Abbot Primate Notker Wolf,
Head of the Benedictine order, Rome